TALES FROM

WITCHWAY

WOOD

CRASH 'N' BANG

TALES FROM
WITCHWAY
WOOD
Crash 'n' Bang

Kaye Umansky

Illustrated by Nick Price

BLOOMSBURY

LONDON BERLIN NEW YORK SYDNEY

For Mo, Ella and the lovely team at Bloomsbury

Bloomsbury Publishing, London, Berlin, New York and Sydney

First published in Great Britain in April 2011 by Bloomsbury Publishing Plc
50 Bedford Square, London, WC1B 3DP

A CIP catalogue record of this book is available from the British Library

ISBN 978 1 4088 0188 8

FSC
www.fsc.org
MIX
Paper from
responsible sources
FSC® C018072

3 5 7 9 10 8 6 4

Typeset by Hewer Text UK Ltd, Edinburgh
Printed in Great Britain by Clays Ltd, St Ives plc, Bungay, Suffolk

www.bloomsbury.com
www.kayeumansky.com

Chapter One

Filth

'And where d'you think you're going?' enquired Witch Sludgegooey. Her head was deep in the oven at the time, but she still heard the door squeak.

'Rehearsal,' mumbled the small Fiend hovering on the doorstep. This was Filth, Sludgegooey's Familiar. He was clearly all set to go. Hair tuft gelled, nails painted black, desperate to be off and away.

'It's not Wednesday, is it?' Sludgegooey emerged from the oven with the tip of her hat on fire. She snatched it off and beat out the flames with a wet dishcloth.

'Extra one. Reviewing the pad.'

'That's musical language, is it? "Reviewing the pad"?'

'Yeah.'

'Meaning?'

'Making a list of what we play. Add some new tunes. Got to keep it fresh, man.'

'Don't call me *man*, Filth. Call me Mistress.'

'OK, Mistress.'

'Don't say OK. Say *yes*.'

'OK then, yeah. Yes.'

'How many times must I tell you? Familiars are supposed to speak *respectfully* to their Witches. Less of the slang. What time will you be back?'

'Dunno. I mean, not sure.'

'Because I could do with a bit of help clearing up.'

Sludgegooey flapped her dishcloth at the mountains of washing-up, deserts of spilt flour and oceans of slimy liquids that urgently awaited attention. She had been baking all day like a mad thing – not because she enjoyed it but because it was the Coven Cake Sale on Saturday. Of course, Filth should have helped, but he had been shut in his room with the radio on, seemingly deaf to her loud knockings and demands for assistance.

'Can't the Broom do it?' suggested Filth.

Sludgegooey's Broom tensed up in its corner, clearly not keen.

'It's too much for the Broom. It can't get inside the oven – it's the wrong shape.'

The Broom gave a sharp nod of agreement. It swept. It flew. It didn't do ovens.

'I'll do it,' promised Filth. 'Soon as I get back.'

'Ah, but *will* you?'

'For real. Yeah. I mean yes, Mistress.'

'Well – all right. But I want you back by midnight.'

'Cool.'

'It might be. I'd take a scarf. You can borrow my spotty one with the egg stain.'

'No, that's all right,' said Filth hastily. 'Look, I gotta split. Laters, yeah?'

'I *beg* your pardon?'

But Filth was already slouching off down the path, snapping his fingers, leaving Sludgegooey pondering once again on the wisdom of choosing a Fiend as a Familiar.

Of course, the real blame lay with the *Find A Familiar* catalogue, which had overstocked on Fiends and was promoting them heavily at the time. They had been described in glowing terms, as follows:

FIENDS

Whizzy, busy little helpers who run around chatter-ing and cooking and putting shelves up whilst you, the Witch, relax on the sofa eating biscuits. Good value on the domestic front. Excellent DIY skills. Trained to assist in all areas of Magic including Incantations,

Cauldron Dancing and Herb Recognition. Next-day delivery. OFFER OF THE MONTH! GET YOURS NOW!

Sludgegooey wasn't domestic and loved slumping around on sofas scoffing biscuits, so that appealed. But it was the *offer of the month* bit that did it because, like all Witches, she loved a bargain. She had sent off for one and waited excitedly for it to arrive and start cooking. She waited . . .

And waited . . .

And waited some more. Finally she complained to the catalogue company, who claimed to have dispatched one ages ago. The man on the phone was quite sniffy and wouldn't apologise, even when Sludgegooey threatened them with her latest curse – a particularly inventive one involving itchy ears, dreams featuring marzipan sharks and the weird smell of burning coming from your shoes.

The sniffy man remained firm. They'd sent one off. Not their fault it hadn't arrived. A bill was in the post.

Sludgegooey said she had no intention of coughing up for a Fiend she didn't have. The sniffy man referred her to the small print, which said she had to. Sludgegooey went into a sulk.

Then – finally – Filth showed up. He had no luggage other than a drum kit, stowed in a number of round boxes that he towed on a handcart. He didn't say where he'd been. When Sludgegooey demanded an explanation, he just shrugged and muttered something about having to see a dude about a thing, then asked to see his bedroom, which he immediately set about painting black and covering with music posters.

That had been a long time ago. And he hadn't changed.

In vain Sludgegooey waited for Filth to whizz, but he didn't. He stood around and leaned against things. He didn't scuttle, he sauntered. He didn't chat, he mumbled. He wasn't at all domestic and his DIY skills were non-existent. You couldn't trust him with the Magical stuff either. He was usually found collapsed in a chair, tapping out rhythms with his eyes closed while cakes caught fire, shelves collapsed and the Brew he was supposed to be watching boiled away to nothing.

He forgot the words to incantations. When he danced round the cauldron, he always added little improvisations of his own, which mucked up the recipe. He got all the herbs wrong because his mind was elsewhere. No, he wasn't a great Familiar. But . . .

Despite everything, Sludgegooey was fond of him.

And secretly rather proud. After all, no other Witch could boast of having a Familiar in an actual band.

'Remember me to the Boys!' she shouted as he disappeared into the trees. She felt a bit rotten about giving him a hard time. She knew he lived for rehearsals. He couldn't wait to be reunited with his drum kit, which he wasn't allowed to keep in the cottage. He would have liked to rehearse every night, but Sludgegooey drew the line at that. As she told him, being a Familiar is not a part-time job. She got tired of making excuses for him in front of the other Witches, who felt she should get a better grip. But . . .

She was fond of him. And she didn't want to stifle his creativity. For when Filth played the drums, he became – well, *Fiendish*. He sparkled. He shone. He whacked, he tapped, he boomed, he smashed, he jug-gled with his drumsticks. He exploded with rhythm and energy. He was on fire. As Sludgegooey said to a friend of hers, if only he put that amount of effort into his other duties, she'd be laughing.

He didn't, though. The friend had been quick to point that out. The friend had gone on to say other negative things about the wisdom of choosing a Fiend for a Familiar. She was that sort of friend. But then, *her* Familiar was a Hamster, so what did she know?

Chapter Two

Arthur

Arthur was in his garden shed, practising scales on his piano. The shed contained a range of garden equipment, all clean and polished and arranged in a tidy row because Arthur was fussy about things like that.

People assume that Dragons live in dirty old caves, but this is not the case. Arthur had no time for caves. Arthur preferred neat bungalows. Properly made-up beds with envelope corners. An orderly kitchen. A table laid with a white cloth and crisp napkins. That's what he liked.

Arthur himself is not that interesting to look at. He is purplish in colour, with a short, purple scaly tail, neatly clipped claws and a set of smallish wings. He has glasses for reading and wears a woolly scarf on cold evenings. Just your average Dragon. The however, is something else. It is Arthur's pride and joy, so let's pause a moment to examine it.

The original instrument had been acquired some years ago from a rubbish dump. The Witch who owned the Dump – Sludgegooey's friend, actually, the one with the Hamster – was fiercely protective of her junk and none too pleased when people helped themselves. She had sent the Hamster round to demand payment. Arthur had had to cough up a fiver, which was far too much, considering the state the piano was in. It was scratched, missing a leg, no pedals, no lid, hopelessly out of tune, half the keys sticking – so Arthur had gone to the library and taken out a book called *Make Your Own Piano*. Sadly, when he arrived home, he realised it was a book about origami. So he had returned it to the library, who made a fuss and claimed that he had scorched one of the pages. Arthur denied this – although, actually, he *had* accidentally dropped a couple of sparks on it. Sparking Up is a Dragon hazard. It can happen at any time. Sneezing can bring it on. Hiccups. Excitement. Or just annoyance at getting out a really useless library book.

Arthur and the librarian had an argument that became quite loud. Readers had looked up from their books and muttered '*Sshh!*' and pointed crossly to the SILENCE sign. The whole unpleasant incident ended with Arthur stumping up yet more money to pay for the damage and marching home, where he set about building a piano from scratch, using only his own brain.

He had hauled the wrecked piano into the shed. He took out the innards and combined them in interesting new ways, using wire and glue and a lot of string. It was fiddly work, but Arthur was patient.

He had gathered up the dismembered piano carcass and glued it back together. He made a new lid for the keyboard. He fashioned a cunning new pair of foot pedals from an old frying pan. He made a little shelf to hold the music. He hung a bucket of water from a hook on the side in case of fire. He made a cart with stout wheels and a cunning little fold-up ramp in order to make the piano easily transportable. He made a stool with a hinged lid to keep the music in. It took *weeks*.

Finally, when it was all finished, he called his mother out to the shed to have a look. She thought it was wonderful.

So. That's Arthur's piano. Be impressed.

Knowing that practice makes perfect, Arthur dutifully ran through his scales every single day. Only when he'd done each one fast, slow, loud, soft and backwards did he finally allow himself to have fun.

That meant flexing his claws, plonking his foot on the loud pedal and bursting into something loud, fast and crashy with a stonking boogie left hand.

This particular evening he was just finishing the hardest scale — the one with all the black notes — when there came a tap at the door.

'Arthur? Can you hear me, lovey?'

'Yes, I can hear you. What is it, Mam?'

'It's gone six, you know.'

'Oh my! Already? I must have got a bit carried away there.'

'I've made us some lovely chilli soup. It's just reached boiling point.'

'Thanks, Mam,' shouted Arthur.

'What about pudding? Would you like some mustard crumble?'

'No time. I've got extra rehearsal tonight, remember?'

'Oh, so you have. Just the soup then?'

'Just the soup. I'll load up the piano and be right in.'

'All right, I'll set out the napkins.'

Arthur liked living with his mother. It was a happy arrangement, as they got on really well. They pottered around the kitchen, chatting and washing up as they went along. Both of them enjoyed good hot meals. Some people have a sweet tooth, but Dragons have a hot tooth. Mustard, chilli, molten lava, roast coal, curry – the hotter the better.

Arthur stood up, closed the lid and set about preparing the piano for its trip through the Wood to the Studio. He did this regularly, so it didn't take long. He had a proper system. It involved pushing it up the ramp on to the cart, securing it with ropes and covering it with a protective blanket, which he fussily secured with clothes pegs.

There. It was all tucked up and ready to go. He would just have time for the soup, then it was off to rehearsal. Tonight, the intention was to review the pad and discuss forthcoming gigs. He hoped the others would be in a good mood. Filth in particular got bored easily when they talked too much instead of playing.

Arthur gave the piano an affectionate pat, shut the shed door and hurried up the path, whistling as he went.

Chapter Three
O'Brian

O'Brian sat at his workbench, hammering nails into the sole of a large battered boot. His small hands were a blur. The sound of the hammer had no pauses, like hail on a flat tin roof.

Taptaptaptapataptaptaptaptaptap . . .

The boot's owner – a big dozy Zombie – stood over him, wiggling the toes of one bare dirty foot, watching the process in admiration. There is something humbling about watching an expert at work.

'There you go, sir,' said O'Brian, slowing down into real time. He held up the mended boot. 'All done.'

'Cor,' said the Zombie. 'That was quick.'

'I'm a Leprechaun. We're fast workers.'

'Yeah? Always thought you was a Pixie.'

'Similar hats,' said O'Brian shortly. 'Common

mistake.' There was another blur of activity, and the boot was suddenly neatly wrapped in brown paper and secured with string. 'That'll be one pound.'

'Amazin',' marvelled the Zombie, taking it. His right thumb came off and dropped on the floor. 'Oops! There she goes again!'

Chuckling ruefully, he bent down, picked it up and dropped it into a pocket to sew back on later. That's the trouble with being a Zombie. Bits fall off.

'Don't want to hurry you,' said O'Brian, 'but I'm closing early. Rehearsal.'

'You boys are playin' for our Reunion Dinner Dance in a coupla weeks,' the Zombie informed him. 'I'm goin', if me legs stay on.'

'Is that so? Well, that'll be something for us both to look forward to, won't it? The pound, if you please.'

After a lot of rummaging, the Zombie finally produced the coin. O'Brian popped it into the left pocket of his red trousers and snatched open the door. The Zombie lurched off down the path.

O'Brian moved out on to the doorstep. His eyes narrowed as the Zombie trod heavily on the wobbly flagstone by the gate – the flagstone that wobbled because *O'Brian kept taking it up to check that his secret pot of gold was still there.*

You need to know about the Pot. In fact, now is a good time to tell you a few things about Leprechauns in general. Here is a useful list.

1. All Leprechauns are a load of cobblers. They traditionally go into shoemaking as a trade. They stay open all hours and never turn a job down. They don't take time off and never go on holiday. Their motto is *The Shoes Won't Wait*.

2. Leprechauns go in for huge families. O'Brian himself has fourteen brothers. Each lives alone in his own workshop. They are forever ringing each other on the spellophone to talk about leather samples and where to go for quality nails.

3. All Leprechauns are very security conscious. This is because they have a *secret pot of gold* buried at the bottom of the garden. They are presented with it at a special coming of age ceremony where there is much feasting and dancing and the occasional bit of bother. They get a long lecture about keeping it safe. In Leprechaun circles, it is considered bad form to allow your Pot to be stolen. After

the ceremony, they are given a map and a packet of sandwiches and ordered to go off into the world and be cobblers.

4. Leprechauns can move *incredibly fast* when they want to.

5. They frequently get mistaken for Pixies. It really annoys them.

That's enough about Leprechauns for now. Oh – except that they're Lucky. All Leprechauns set great store by Luck. Their gardens are awash with shamrock and four-leafed clover. Of course, they know you can't rely *solely* on Luck. Luck is a tricky thing. Sometimes, other people's luck can be your misfortune. All the shamrock in the world won't stop people trying to nick your gold, so you have to be practical and take the proper precautions.

The Zombie moved on and O'Brian breathed again.

Right! Time to get ready! He gave a jolly little skip on the spot, then glanced furtively over his shoulder, hoping nobody had seen. Leprechauns have an unfortunate tendency to caper about in a pointy-toed, uncool way that reminds people of dewy meadows and Fairy rings. It is embarrassing and O'Brian is trying to cut it out, but sometimes his feet just rise up and do their thing.

Back inside, he hurried through the workshop, whipping off his apron as he went. The shop smelled of leather and was full of tiny tools and jars of nails and glue. There were shelves lined with neatly labelled shoeboxes – some huge, some really small. O'Brian catered for everybody from tiny Fairies to thumping great GIANTS, with a lot of other weird types in between.

At the back of the shop was a small living area with a bed, a wardrobe and a small stove, where O'Brian cooked his supper and made up vast vats of shoe glue.

He hurried to his bed, reached under his pillow and drew out a long, thin metal box. He opened the lid. Inside, on a bed of velvet, lay his whistle. The traditional Leprechaun penny whistle, handed down through many generations.

Leprechaun families produce only one good musician per generation – in this case, O'Brian. His brothers all possessed cloth ears, whereas he had been able to pick out recognisable tunes on a hollow twig from the word go. So it was only right that he inherited the whistle. Of course, if truth be known, he would have preferred a saxophone. But you make the best of what you're given.

He picked up the whistle, gave it a brisk wipe on his sleeve and placed it to his lips.

Toodly-tiddly-weedly-wee, toodly-tiddly wheeee!
Tiddly-toodly-idio, fiddly-foodly-pheeeee!

The merry little tune burst out and scampered around the rafters – and instantly, his Leprechaun side took over. His knees began to piston up and down while his feet performed a lot of intricate footwork with much unnecessary waving.

Darn! He *must* stop doing that.

He lowered the whistle, anchored his feet to the floor and concentrated.

Must not skip, thought O'Brian. *Must not skip.*

Finally under control, he marched to the wardrobe, threw open the door and examined his reflection in the long mirror. Green hat. Green jerkin. Red trousers. Beautiful soft boots with curly toes. Sandy eyebrows, matching ginger beard. Penny whistle. Yep, he looked like a Leprechaun.

O'Brian sighed. Looking like a Leprechaun was no good.

He pushed the hat further down over his eyes, undid the top three buttons of his jerkin, sucked in his cheeks and arranged his features into an expression of what he hoped was brooding menace. He hung the whistle round his neck. Originally it had come with a green ribbon, but at Filth's suggestion O'Brian had replaced it with a black leather thong, which looked much cooler.

There. That was better. Now he looked a bit more like a Leprechaun in a Crash 'n' Bang band. A Leprechaun with attitude. The sort of Leprechaun that girls might give the eye to, once they'd given up on Filth.

It was then that the spellophone rang.

O'Brian hesitated. He knew who it would be. It would be one of his brothers. Seamus or Kieran or Niall or Dillon or Paddy or – well, any of them. They would want to talk about insoles and the best brand of shoelaces.

Should he answer?

No. Not tonight. He could do without another lecture. His brothers didn't understand why he wanted to be in a band. They thought it was an un-Leprechaunish hobby that would get him nowhere. They would try and make him feel guilty about closing early and going off to enjoy himself when he should be at home cobbling.

After ringing exactly fourteen times, the spellophone fell silent. O'Brian let out his breath in a little explosion of relief.

He hurried to the door, stepped out, shut it, locked

it, checked it, pocketed the key, ran a few steps down the path, ran back, checked it again. Then he scurried down the garden path and stood on the wobbly flagstone, which jiggled a bit. Carefully, O'Brian stamped it flat and fluffed up the surrounding clumps of shamrock which were there for protection and disguise. There. That was better.

Automatically, he glanced up at the Rainbow Deflector on the workshop roof. This was a complicated wire contraption mounted on a pole, with spokes and rods and wheels and a large dish. It was currently at ease. No rainbows after sundown, of course. (Leprechauns have a dread of rainbows, which indicate where gold is buried. Most have Deflectors on their roofs. As a bonus, they get good spellovision reception.)

Happy that all was secure, O'Brian went into overdrive! He stood on the tip of one curly-toed boot, pulled in his elbows, breathed in deeply – and began to skip. Knees pumping, feet flashing, faster, faster, faster, until he was nothing but a confusing blur.

Then he vanished! Disappeared, just like that! The air wobbled, a small wind swept down the path, the gate opened and banged shut. After a moment, there came a brief snatch of a faraway tune played on a penny whistle – then silence.

On a high, lonely mountain to the north of Witchway Wood, a tall shadowy figure stands poised in the entrance to a deep dark cave . . . hairy face raised, sniffing the air, yellow eyes staring up at the darkening sky . . . searching, searching for the moon . . .

Chapter Four

TT

'Gareth,' said the Thing in the Moonmad T-shirt, addressing its pet, who lived in a bowl on the sideboard. 'I am in despair.'

Gareth said nothing, because he was a goldfish.

Outside, night was descending. Stars were coming out, and so were the owls – along with Witches, Trolls, Yetis, Ghosts, Goblins, Zombies, Gnomes, Mummies and all the other assorted types that for the sake of simplicity can fall under the heading of Monsters. Witchway Wood is a mixed area. A lot of unusual folk live there and night always brings them Out.

The Thing in the Moonmad T-shirt wasn't Out, though. It was definitely In. In a chair, in a hole, in the mossy bank where it lived. In, and peering dolefully at the Situations Vacant column in *The Daily Miracle* by the light of a guttering candle.

This was unusual. The Thing wasn't much of a homebody. It liked to be where the action was, not slumped and sighing in a chair.

Most people call the Thing just that – the Thing. They don't even give him a gender, usually referring to him as 'It'. His friends, however, know him as TT, know he is a boy and never give him pink T-shirts on his birthday. Not that they ever give him much anyway. Certainly not anything he could actually *do* with, like money.

TT was small and hairy with two protruding teeth and two big, flapping ears. The T-shirt was a washed-out black colour and the Moonmad lettering was peeling off. It was fraying round the neck. A bit itchy. Shrunken. Not nice. It matched its wearer's mood.

'What shall I do, Gareth?' went on TT. 'There's nothing in the paper again. I'm getting desperate.'

Indeed, he was. He'd been out of work for weeks and was feeling the pinch. Right now the larder contained nothing but a packet of fish food, half a banana and the last tin of Stringy Thingy Noodles. Not only was he running low on food, there were a lot of other problems as well. He was behind with the rent. He was out of soap. The spellovision was on the blink. He couldn't afford any more T-shirts, although he'd seen a purple one he really wanted. Worst of all, he couldn't raise the money for his weekly trip to the cinema. TT loved the movies. Scott Sinister's latest blockbuster was showing. Finding employment was imperative.

The trouble was, there were only two jobs on offer in the Situations Vacant column. One was for a Brain Surgeon and the other was for a Lady's Companion.

'It's not that I'm fussy,' said TT, lowering the paper. 'I can turn my hand to most things. You know that. I've delivered papers, handed out fliers, been a chauffeur, a butler, a tea boy, worked in spellovision, been a cave rescuer. Mind you, they were all dead end.'

Plop! Gareth blew a sympathetic bubble to show he was listening.

TT picked up the paper again and re-examined the jobs. He would certainly have had a crack at the Brain Surgery. After all, how hard could it be? The trouble was that they wanted you to bring a full set of scalpels and were asking to see some sort of certificate which he didn't have. He could have a go at forging the certificate, perhaps, but the scalpels were another matter.

Being a Lady's Companion was out of the question, because he didn't possess a frock. All he had were Moonmad T-shirts. Besides, he couldn't see himself sitting in armchairs drinking flowers or eating bonnets or whatever it was Lady's Companions did.

Hmm. Problems.

His eyes wandered down the page, half of which was taken up with a large advertisement. He brightened up a bit.

'Hey! See this?' TT held the paper in front of Gareth, forgetting that being a fish with eyes on two sides, he couldn't. 'There's a big outdoor music festival in Sludgehaven-on-Sea next Saturday. "*The Battle of the Bands*", they're calling it.'

TT was a music lover. He liked music almost as much as the pictures.

'Says it's being held in a big field just outside the town,' he went on. 'The best band gets a hundred pounds and a recording contract with *Genie Sounds*. That's the new record label that's being started up by Ali Pali, remember? I read about it in the paper. Imagine! A hundred pounds, Gareth! What we could do with that. It says "*Mystery Celebrities on the judging panel*". I wonder who they are? I fancy a trip to Sludgehaven. A day in the sun, listening to music. What could be nicer? The tickets are five pounds each. It says "*Book now to avoid disappointment*".'

Gareth blew a stream of stern bubbles. They clearly contained a warning.

'Yes, I know,' sighed TT. 'I *know* we've got no money.'

He flung the paper to one side and stared around the hole, which urgently needed attention. The walls were crumbling away and there was a nasty crack in the ceiling. Piles of earth were dotted around and growing daily. Subsidence. Hmm. More money.

So now what? He should shovel the earth up really, but he wasn't in the mood. He could open the noodles, but what would he eat tomorrow? Watching spello was out until he could afford to get it fixed. What to do? What to do?

Perhaps a walk was in order. A bit of fresh air, that was the ticket. It would save on candles. Maybe he would find a set of scalpels on a grass verge, dropped by some passing Brain Surgeon. Anyway, sitting around brooding got you nowhere.

More cheerful now that he had a plan of action, TT rose, hurried to his T-shirt drawers and pored over the options.

TT took his Moonmad T-shirts seriously. There were three drawers full of them in various colours (except pink). All neatly folded and graded in a proper system. Top drawer: newest ones, all crisp and ready for the good times. Next drawer down: the well loved ones he wore indoors when he wasn't expecting visitors. In the bottom drawer were the old clapped-out ones he used for the bad times and decorating.

After a moment or two, TT made his decision. Yellow. A nice, bright, optimistic, sunny yellow one, for the start of Great New Things.

Freshly attired, he crossed over to the sideboard and tapped gently on the glass.

'I'm off out, Gareth. See you in a bit.'

Gareth blew a supportive bubble.

On the way out, TT grabbed the *Miracle* and stuffed it under his arm. If no scalpels were lying around, he would find a quiet glade and do the crossword puzzle. You had to keep the brain active. Maybe he would come up with an idea. Some sort of exciting new business venture. Something that he could really get his teeth into. That would be good.

Somewhere deep in Witchway Wood, where no birds sing, a tall dark shape slinks along, keeping in the shadows of the trees . . .

Chapter Five

Rehearsal

'So,' said Arthur briskly. 'We've got the Marching Around tune, the Basic Barn Dance tune, the Wedding tune, the Happy Birthday tune, the All-Purpose Overture and the Clear-Off-The-Show's-Over tune. Is that it?'

The Boys were gathered in the Studio. This was a small shed lined with egg boxes to keep the noise in. Sadly, a team of cowboy Goblins had done the job and stuck the boxes on the outside, which wasn't quite as effective, particularly after the first heavy rainfall. Also, when the Boys were playing it usually got unbearably hot and stuffy, so they left the door ajar. Soundproof it wasn't.

Filth sat slumped on his drum stool, picking at his nail varnish. O'Brian had just arrived in a wobble of air and was currently collapsed against the wall, fanning himself and getting his breath back. Arthur leaned on the piano lid, writing a list with a pencil, looking efficient.

'There's the Jaunty Jig,' said O'Brian, finding his breath.

'Jaunty Jig,' said Arthur, noting it down.

'*Jig*,' muttered Filth. 'Huh.'

'Always goes down well,' said O'Brian. He just stopped himself adding 'Especially my solo', although he thought it.

Arthur ran his pencil down the list. 'Seven basic numbers. That's what we've got. We need more. I think we should add a Waltz. The Skeletons kept requesting it at their last dance. I thought they were going to storm the stage.'

'Oh, man,' muttered Filth. 'A *Waltz*? Man.'

'Problems, Filth?' asked Arthur tiredly. He knew what was coming.

'Are you serious? A *Waltz*. I mean. It's not cool, dude.'

'I know,' said Arthur. 'I *know*. But sadly, we have to play what people want. We've got to earn a living. Well, some of us do. We don't all have a secret pot of Leprechaun gold buried in our garden.'

'We don't *open* it,' explained O'Brian wearily. 'I've

told you a hundred times. It's not for spending. It's just *there*.' This was true. For Leprechauns, the whole point of having a pot of gold is, well, having a pot of gold.

'But we're not in it for the bread,' went on Filth. 'We've got day jobs for that. The music's for love, dude.'

'Even so, we have to play what people like,' said Arthur. 'It's a tough world out there.'

'But I don't *like* what people like. I wanna play Crash 'n' Bang.'

'We all do! But life is full of compromise, Filth. And it's not as though we don't ever play the good stuff, is it? What about that number we came up with the other week? With the boogie bass in the left hand? When we jammed for hours non-stop? Remember?'

'Yeah, but we only play like that in rehearsals,' complained Filth. 'Never in public.'

'That's because the public doesn't *like* it.'

'Yeah, but *I* do. Anyway, I'm fed up with talking. I want to play.' Filth picked up his drumsticks.

'Good,' said Arthur. 'Because we've got a Zombie Reunion Dinner Dance coming up Saturday week and they're asking for a Lurching tune. So we should get cracking if we're going to do a Waltz as well.'

Filth put down the sticks, folded his arms and

looked mutinous. These little disagreements came up from time to time. It happens with creative types.

'Right,' said Arthur, ignoring him. 'Think lurchy.' He put down his pencil, sat at the piano and flexed his claws. 'I thought something like this.'

And he began to play something lurchy. It had a thumpy, lumpy sort of left hand, with long pauses between thumps. His right claw added a series of sinister sounding chords on the top. After a moment, O'Brian joined in with some jolly little toodles that sounded more like Skipping Pixies than Lurching Zombies.

Arthur stopped.

'Perhaps a little less jaunty, O'Brian. Less village green and more foggy graveyard.'

'You want me to play like fog?'

'Yes.'

O'Brian attempted to play like fog. It still sounded a bit toodly. Arthur added a few lurchy thumps on the piano. After a moment or two, they lurched and fogged to a ragged halt.

'It's not working,' said Filth, still sulking. 'I don't like it.'

'No?' said Arthur politely. 'Oh dear. Would you sooner start with the Waltz, then?'

'No.'

'Well, what, then?'

'This,' said Filth. And he closed his eyes and began tapping out a little rhythm on the rim of his side drum.

It was a simple little rhythm, but my, was it infectious! It instantaneously made your feet tap. *Tee-tata-tee-tata-tee-tata-tee!* Then the bass drum joined in. *Boom! Boom! Boom! Boom!* Then the cymbal. *Tsssk! Tssssk! Tssk, tssk, tsssk!*

After a moment, Arthur's head began to nod in time. Then he gave a little chuckle, spat on his claws and hunched over the keys. His left claw crashed into action, moving up and down the keyboard, thumping out the bass. His right claw added choppy little chords that fitted in all the right places. His tail swished rhythmically from side to side.

O'Brian raised his whistle to his lips and anchored himself to the spot, determined not to break into unwanted skipping. For some days, a delicious little melody had been capering at the back of his mind and now was the time to try it out.

His nimble fingers moved up and down as he blew. Out came the tricky little tune. It crept into the ear and danced around inside the head, fitting in perfectly.

Yes, together, they sounded *good*. This was the

sort of stuff they liked to play. Feel-good, stomp-ing, wave-your-arms-around sort of music. And above all, *loud*. Arthur's piano was capable of mak-ing a terrific din and so were Filth's drums – and around them both O'Brian wove his catchy little melody. Sparks exploded from Arthur's nostrils. Filth's hair gel began melting and trickling down his face. O'Brian was scarlet with the effort of control-ling his twitching feet.

Tee-tata-tee-tata, boom, boom boom! Honka-tonka, honka-tonka, twiddly tweedly woo!

'Bring it down!' shouted Arthur, and suddenly they were all playing quietly, like thieves in the night.

'Let it go!' roared Arthur, after a minute or two of this. And they let it go, like a storm in the mountains!

TEE-TATA-CRASH! HONKETTY-TONKETTY-TONK! WHEE-TIDDLY-WHEE!

Sweat dripped, sparks sparkled, drumsticks flashed in the air. It was so loud, a train could have roared past and they wouldn't have heard.

Of course, it couldn't go on for ever. This was high-energy stuff and at some point they would have to stop for a breather. Finally, at a signal from Arthur, it all ended on a gigantic, triumphant crash, causing the walls to tremble and a number of soggy egg boxes to dislodge and slither off the roof.

'Yeah, baby!' cried Filth, throwing his sticks in the air and catching them deftly in one hand. 'That's what I'm *talking* about!'

Arthur fished around in his piano stool for the towel he kept there to wipe his face and O'Brian snatched off his hat and fanned himself. All three were grinning broadly.

'Now *that's* what I call music,' said an unexpected voice from the doorway.

It was the Thing in the Moonmad T-shirt.

Chapter Six

A Proposal

'Really?' said Arthur. He was somewhat taken aback. The Studio was in a remote part of the Wood. The few visitors who showed up at the door had usually walked miles to demand that they keep the noise down. 'You liked it?'

'Liked it?' cried TT, stepping in and closing the door behind him. 'I loved it! I was just passing by, feeling a bit fed up, you know? But you've perked me up, you have. You and your wild and crazy sounds. Wow. You boys are *good*.'

'Oh. Well, thanks very much,' said Arthur. 'Much appreciated. We call it Crash 'n' Bang. It's not for everybody. Er – can I help you?'

'Actually,' said TT, 'I was thinking that I might be able to help *you*.'

'If you want us to do a gig, we're booked up for the next month,' said Arthur. 'Sorry.'

'I'm not surprised,' said TT. 'Skeleton weddings, Zombie dinner dances, Witch pantomimes. Do 'em all, don't you?'

'Worse luck,' said Filth under his breath. Arthur shot him an impatient look and he gave a little shrug and began picking at his nail varnish again.

'They should pay you more,' said TT. 'Talent like yours shouldn't come cheap.'

'I get the best rate I can,' said Arthur rather stiffly.

'Of course you do,' agreed TT hastily. 'I'm just saying you deserve more. I'm a big fan of you boys. I was at your first ever gig. When everything went wrong and all the drums got punctured.'

Filth gave a little shudder. He didn't want to be reminded of their first gig – a Witch Talent Contest that had ended in a full-scale riot. Come to think of it, a lot of their gigs ended in riots. People seemed to enjoy the fighting more than the music.

'I asked for your autographs,' went on TT. 'You might remember.'

Everyone looked blank. Their memories of the disastrous occasion included nothing as flattering as being asked for an autograph.

'You've improved a lot since then,' said TT. 'I

mean, a *lot*. Of course, it's a pity about the sort of rubbish they make you play. Old-fashioned, isn't it? Marches and jigs and whatnot.'

'Yes, well, that's what's popular, I'm afraid,' said Arthur.

'I know,' agreed TT sympathetically. 'No taste at all, the types who live around here. Cloth-eared, every last one of 'em.'

'Right!' chorused the Boys.

'All that boring old stuff. You're better than that.'

'We are!'

'You know what you've got? Raw talent. With decent management, you could go far.'

'Right!' yelled Filth and O'Brian. Only Arthur didn't join in.

'Actually,' he said shortly, '*I* manage us.'

'Oh, I know,' soothed TT. 'And you do a great job, I can see that. As far as it goes. You get the gigs, collect the money, all that. Somebody's got to do it. Must eat into your creative time, though. Your essential *piano-playing* time.'

'Well – yes, it does, a bit,' agreed Arthur. It did. The band generated a lot of paperwork.

'You're a musician, right?'

'Well, yes, but someone has to –'

'You just want to make Crash 'n' Bang music. Live the dream.'

'Yes, but –'

'A big stage. A wild crowd. That's what you boys live for.'

'Yes, but –'

'Arthur.' TT held up a small hairy hand, stopping him in his tracks. 'You're not seeing the big picture. Hear me out.' He pulled *The Daily Miracle* from under his arm. 'There's an interesting piece in the paper you might like to see. And I've got a little proposal I'd like to put to you . . .'

A branch snaps, some bushes rustle – and the tall dark shape emerges from the trees. Crouching low, it creeps towards the weeping willow tree that grows next to the Studio. It parts the branches and ducks beneath . . .

Chapter Seven

Time Off

It was the following morning and Sludgegooey sat in her kitchen, surrounded by the wreckage from the day before. Things were even worse because the mess from breakfast was now added to it. She was irritably eating an egg while her Broom barged about the place, sweeping up in a slapdash fashion and looking put out.

Filth came shuffling into the room in his nightshirt. The Broom swept a pile of dirt into his path on purpose, then banged itself up against the wall.

'You're up, then,' snapped Sludgegooey. 'I put your egg on to boil an hour ago.'

'Cool,' yawned Filth.

'No. Hot, actually. It exploded. You'll have to scrape it off the walls. What time did you get in last night?'

'Dunno.'

'It was past midnight, wasn't it? No wonder you're up so late. I thought you said you'd clear up the kitchen.'

'I will,' said Filth. 'I *will.*'

'You said that yesterday. The Broom's fed up with you, and so am I. This won't do. It won't do at all.'

'Something came up,' muttered Filth. He reached for a spoon and began tapping on the table edge. Sludgegooey stared at him. He seemed a bit tense. Not quite himself. Like he had something to say but was reluctant to come out with it.

'What?' demanded Sludgegooey. 'Come on, spit it out.'

'Got ourselves a new manager.'

'A *new manager*? I thought Arthur did all that sort of thing. Stop tapping – it's driving me mad.' Sludgegooey leaned across and snatched away the spoon.

'He does. Did. Not any more.'

'Well, come on then, tell me. Who is this new manager?'

'The Thing.'

'What – in the Moonmad T-shirt?'

'Yeah.'

'I'd be careful,' said Sludgegooey darkly. 'Never holds a job for more than two minutes, that one. Plenty of enthusiasm but no staying power. What does the Thing do that Arthur doesn't?'

'Gotta lotta new ideas. New gear for a start. New image.'

'Is that all?'

'Publicity. Posters. Going to start up a fan club. Dolls, maybe.'

'Dolls? What – of *you*?'

'Yeah. Oh, and he's got us, like, this big gig.' Filth announced this with a casual air that didn't deceive Sludgegooey.

'What big gig?'

'Battle of the Bands. It's a music festival. We're, like, entering.'

'Is that so? And where is this *Battle* to be fought?'

Filth muttered something under his breath and nervously picked up a fork.

'Where? Speak up.' Sludgegooey leaned over and snatched it away.

'Sludgehaven-on-Sea.'

'But that's miles away!'

'Not that far.'

'Yes it is, it's miles. Remember when we went there on holiday with the Coven that time? On a coach?'

'Yeah,' said Filth, who did. It had been an eventful journey. In fact, it had been an eventful holiday. Holidays with Witches always are.

'Remember the show on the pier?' Sludgegooey went all nostalgic. 'And when we turned the landlady into a chicken?'*

'Yeah,' said Filth.

'Yes, we had a good time, despite that ridiculous No Magic rule they've got. Nice and sunny, never a drop of rain. But I do know it took ages to get there. When is this nonsense supposed to take place?'

'On Saturday.'

'It's the Cake Sale on Saturday. I hope you're not expecting time off.'

'Well – yeah.' Filth looked anxious. 'Man. Come on. It's, like, our big break. We get to play our kinda sounds to a big crowd for once. Show what we can do.'

'I suppose by *your kinda sounds* you mean that horrible thump and smash stuff?'

'Crash 'n' Bang,' said Filth. 'It's called Crash 'n'

* Footnote. Anyone who has read *Pongwiffy and the Holiday of Doom* can't help but remember *that* trip.

Bang. You know that.'

'All I know is, it's a racket. It hasn't even got any words to sing along with. Just a lot of noise.'

Filth chose to ignore this. They had been down this road before, many times.

'Look,' he said. 'Look, I'll only be gone for one night. Leave on Friday, back late Saturday. Or maybe Sunday. Sunday morning at the latest.'

'Think again,' said Sludgegooey and went back to her egg. There was a pause. Filth said casually, 'Yep. Back Sunday morning. With the cheque.'

'Cheque?' Sludgegooey sat up.

'Yep. There's a prize. A cheque and a recording contract with *Genie Sounds*. Ali Pali's starting up a record label. Looking for talent. That's what the Battle's all about.'

'Never mind Ali Pali, go back to the cheque. How big a cheque?'

'A hundred pounds.'

'What, *each*? Or divided between you? Think carefully, this is important.'

'I dunno. Who cares? The main thing's the recording contract.'

Sludgegooey didn't think so, but didn't want to spoil his dreams. Well, not yet. If he didn't win, him and his dreams were toast.

'How many bands are entering?' she asked.

'Dunno.'

'Reckon you'll win?'

'Are you serious?' Filth stared at her, amazed. 'Like, *yeah*.'

'Because I could put a curse on the competition if you want. Just to make sure.'

'*No!*' cried Filth, horrified. 'This is *music*!'

'Just a little one. They'd never know.'

'No! *No!*'

'Well, have it your own way. But you'd better win.'

'So I can go?'

'All right. Just this once, I'll give you the time off. Of course, I'm entitled to a cut of the money for letting you go.'

'Whatever.' Filth shrugged. 'Take it all, I don't care.'

'All right then, I will,' said Sludgegooey quickly. 'You can put that on paper and sign it. You leave on Friday, you say?'

'Yeah. Got stuff to do, mind. Got lunch later today with TT.'

'You're having lunch with tea?' Sludgegooey was confused.

'No, TT. The Thing.'

'How long is that going to take?'

'Be a while. There's a lot to sort out. I'd stay and help clean the kitchen but . . .'

'That's all right,' said Sludgegooey. 'You sit and practise your tapping and I'll do you another egg. You have to get your strength up if you're going to bring home that cheque.' She glared at the Broom. 'I'll use it to buy a decent vacuum cleaner.'

'Mam?' shouted Arthur through the bedroom door.

There was a long pause. Then a sleepy voice called, 'Yeeeees?'

'Are you taking a nap?'

'Well, I was.'

'I'm off to lunch shortly. Meeting up with the new manager.'

'That's lovely.'

'I've burnt you some toast. It's on a tray in the kitchen.'

'All right.'

'I might be late. There's a lot to discuss.'

'All right, son. You enjoy yourself.'

'You remember I'll be away on Friday?'

'Yes.'

'Want me to get anything in?'

'No, I'll be all right. Don't you worry about me.'

Dragon mums are very easy-going.

O'Brian sat on a bench in his workshop, mopping his brow and getting his breath back. He had been in overdrive since sunrise, completing what would normally have been a week's work in record time. The shelves groaned under the weight of a thousand shoeboxes. His apron was off and his tools were put away. The *Closed* sign was up. It was goodbye cobbling, hello new career!

O'Brian hugged himself, thinking of all that lay ahead. Lunch in a café – that'd be a first. A trip to the coast. Playing in the Battle of the Bands. *Winning* the Battle of the Bands. And then – a whole new life. Stadiums. Hotels. Screaming fans. Fame. Travel. He would be living the Crash 'n' Bang dream. Of course, his brothers would disapprove, but sometimes you just had to follow your heart.

The spellophone rang. Oh. That would be one of them, no doubt. Should he answer?

No. Best keep quiet about the trip to Sludgehaven. Right now, he could do without brotherly disapproval. They would pour cold water on his dreams. Try and make him stay home and cobble.

After fourteen rings, the spellophone fell silent. O'Brian was just about to relax when there came a gentle knock on the door.

'Yes? What?' shouted O'Brian. Was he never to be left in peace?

'Please, sweet darling cobbler, will you mend my shoes?' came a tiny voice. It sounded like silver bells played under starlight next to a rippling brook.

If the voice was anything to go by, it was obviously a Fairy. A beautiful little Fairy with delicate wings and a gauzy dress, holding a minuscule pair of glass slippers in her hand. Who could resist?

'No!' shouted O'Brian. 'Away with you. I'm closed.'

'But I'm a Fairy,' said the silver voice.

'So? I'm a Leprechaun!'

'I heard you were a Pixie.'

'*Similar hat!*'

'No need to shout. Whatever you are, you're a cobbler, aren't you?'

'*Was* a cobbler. I'm having a change of career.'

'You're supposed to help Fairies,' said the voice, not quite so silvery now. 'You're supposed to do anything we ask. Then, if we feel like it, we graciously give you three wishes.'

'And what would I want with three wishes?' scoffed O'Brian. 'You can keep 'em! I've got the Luck of the Leprechauns. I'm off to win the Battle of the Bands and get a recording contract!'

'Is that so?' The voice was really frosty now. 'Well,

I wouldn't rely on it. Not with that attitude.'

'And I suppose you think *you* know about music?' sneered O'Brian.

'Well, yes,' snapped the Fairy. 'As a matter of fact, I think I do.'

'*Little People* music,' jeered O'Brian. 'That's what you lot like. Well, I've moved on, see. I play Crash 'n' Bang. That's not for the likes of you Fairies.'

'Why not?'

'Because you wouldn't get it. Soppy *tippy-toe* music, that's more your line.'

'Well, that just goes to show how little you know. Now, about these shoes . . .'

'Ah, get back to yer mushroom!' roared O'Brian. 'Fix your own daft little shoes!'

There was a shocked silence.

'Anyway,' came the icy voice after a bit, 'anyway, you've lost the good will of the Fairies.'

'So? Leprechaun Luck cancels out Fairy Magic any time.'

'I think you'll find it doesn't.'

'It does so. Away with you, I say!'

'You'll be sorry about this,' said the Fairy ominously.

'Oh, will I? I don't *think* so. Go waggle your wings and don't come bothering me again.'

There came the sound of tiny footsteps crossly

pattering away.

'Attaboy!' said O'Brian to himself. 'Told a Fairy to get lost. That's Crash 'n' Bang.' He gave a little chuckle and began undoing the top three buttons of his jerkin. For some reason, they didn't want to undo. He fought with them for ages, but the holes seemed to have shrunk or something.

That was only the beginning of his troubles.

Far away on a mountain, from inside the dark cave there comes a faint scratching sound. If you listen carefully, you will recognise it. It is the sound of . . .

Scribbling?

Chapter Eight
Lunch

The cafe was a popular place with the residents of Witchway Wood, mainly because it was cheap. It was called *Tea And Chips* and was owned and run by the Yeti Brothers. Their names were Spag Yeti and Conf Yeti and they were large, hairy and rude to the customers, who they despised. Spag manned the tea urn. Conf chopped chips and fried them in grease. Both of them took turns in taking the money and being rude. It was a system that worked.

Right now the cafe was empty, but shortly the lunchtime rush would begin and it would be seething.

TT, wearing another crisp new Moonmad T-shirt today, in confident red, marched up to the counter. He was carrying a briefcase and had a spring in his step. Spag was measuring out tea and Conf was slicing potatoes. Both of them had their backs turned.

'Not-a open,' snarled Spag over his shoulder.

'I know,' said TT. 'I just want to reserve a table for four.'

'Oh yeah? You theenk-a thees posh hotel?'

'I'll pay extra,' said TT importantly. 'In fact, I'll pay double if you put a *Private Function* notice on the door. I've got a business meeting, you see. We need a bit of quiet. To talk.'

Spag and Conf exchanged glances. They knew about the Thing's reduced circumstances.

'You got-a money?' enquired Spag suspiciously.

'Certainly.' TT patted his pocket, which duly clinked. 'I've gone into Music Management. I've moved up in the world.' He stared around loftily. 'In fact, I don't suppose you'll see me again, not after today. I'll be dining in places where they put *flowers* on the table instead of grease. I'm only slumming it here because it's late notice. Do we have a deal or not?'

'OK,' said Spag. 'You pay double, is-a deal. *CHI-I-I-IP?*' This last word was roared.

'Yes, please,' said TT humbly, dropping the lordly manner. The half banana hadn't been much of a breakfast. He'd dearly love a chip.

'Not-a you,' sneered Conf as a bullet-shaped head

poked out from the door behind the counter. It belonged to a very short, squat Troll wearing a soaking wet apron and a pair of yellow rubber gloves. In one hand, he held a dripping dishmop.

'Uh?' said the Troll called Chip.

'Priveet-a Function notice. Steek it out,' instructed Spag.

'Uh.'

'And fetch-a more potatoes,' added Conf.

'Uh,' said Chip. And disappeared again. He reappeared with a large square piece of cardboard and waddled to the door. He was so short, his knuckles dragged on the ground. But he was wide. His bald head was set directly on his huge shoulders, without a sign of neck.

'New dishwasher?' enquired TT.

'Yeah,' said Spag.

'Does he say anything else but Uh?'

'No. He speak-a Trolleesh. Ees-a one-word-a language. What it to you?'

'Oh, nothing. We'll take this table by the window,' said TT, pulling out a chair. He peered down at the filthy tabletop and set the briefcase on the floor, where it stuck.

'Menu!' growled Spag, slapping down a scrap of old cardboard with *TEA AND CHEEPSA* scrawled on it. 'What time-a your rubbeesh so-called-a *beeesi-ness* friends-a come?'

'Soon,' said TT, staring through the dirty window. 'In fact, here's one now.'

Arthur came bustling up the track with a large folder under his arm. He arrived at the door at the same time as Chip, who was hanging up the notice. Arthur tried to squeeze by but Chip wasn't having any of it. There was a bit of a stand-off.

'It's all right, you can let him in,' called TT. 'He's with me.'

Chip shuffled to one side and waved a yellow-gloved hand.

'Thank you so much,' said Arthur politely to Chip.

'Uh,' said Chip politely to Arthur.

Arthur entered, stared around, grimaced, pulled out a chair, sat down, inspected the tabletop, produced a paper hanky, spread it out fussily and opened his folder.

'Right,' he said. 'I've got the band accounts here, and a list of forthcoming gigs. I thought we could run through the diary before –'

'Ah, we needn't bother ourselves about that,' said TT breezily. 'All that's in the past. From now on, it's a new style of management. We've got to get you ready for the big time. The Battle on Saturday. That's what we need to concentrate on. Forget the local gigs — they're all small stuff.'

'Well, yes, but the Zombie Reunion's coming up —'

'I cancelled it.'

'You *cancelled* it?'

'Yep. Ah. Here comes the drummer.'

Filth came strolling through the trees, head in the clouds and fingers snapping as usual. He arrived at the door and came face to face with Chip, who now had two enormous sacks of potatoes balanced on his broad shoulders.

'He's in the band,' called TT. 'Let him pass, please, Chip.'

'Uh,' said Chip to Filth, waving him in.

'Hey!' said Filth. 'No, dude, after *you*. I'll get the door.'

Chip waddled in, carrying the sacks as easily as if they were full of feathers. Arthur, TT and Filth watched in awe as he disappeared round the back.

'Strong,' said Arthur.

'Way strong,' agreed Filth.

'Mmm,' said TT thoughtfully.

'O'Brian not here yet?' enquired Filth, throwing himself into a chair.

There was a wobble of air around the fourth chair.

'Yep,' said a voice. 'I am.'

And there was O'Brian, looking hot and bothered. One of his fingers was bandaged and he had a swollen eye.

'What's up with the digit, dude?' asked Filth.

'Shut it in the door.'

'And the eye?' asked Arthur.

'Slipped on a chisel,' mumbled O'Brian. 'Banged it on the workbench.'

This was true. But what he *didn't* say was that the chisel had mysteriously lifted itself off a hook and dropped on the floor right under his foot. And the door had slammed itself shut on purpose – or so it had seemed. Other things had gone wrong as well: a lost door key, curdled milk, ants in the larder, a boiled-dry kettle. A whole series of annoying little accidents and misfortunes, starting with the buttons, which he still couldn't undo.

'Ready to order?' growled Conf from behind the counter.

'Yes,' said TT. 'We're all here now. What'll you have, boys? Anything you like – it's on me.'

'Tea, I think,' said Arthur. 'With chips on the side. Do you have chilli sauce, by any chance?' Conf gave him a Look. 'Oh, all right, just chips then.'

'Chips for me, man,' said Filth. 'And tea to wash it down.'

'What about-a the Peexie?' asked Conf. O'Brian went into a sulk.

'He's not a Pixie, he's a Leprechaun,' explained Arthur. 'Similar hat.'

'All-a the same to me. What he having?'

'Come on, O'Brian,' sighed Filth. He pushed over the menu. 'Choose, man.'

O'Brian rarely ate out and when he did he didn't like to be rushed, particularly by a Yeti who confused him with a Pixie.

'Now then,' he pondered. 'What shall it be? I could have tea. On the other hand, I could have chips. Decisions, decisions. Of course, I could go mad and have tea *and* chips —'

'Four teas and chips,' TT told Conf. 'Right. Let's get started. I've been making enquiries. Here's the deal. Today's Wednesday. We leave early on Friday in the band van. That gives us today and tomorrow to prepare.'

'What band van?' interrupted Arthur. 'We don't have a van.'

'You can leave that to me,' said TT breezily. 'Trust me. I'm the manager. There'll be a van. If we don't stop, we can make it to Sludgehaven by sundown.'

'That's pushing it, isn't it?' said Arthur. He had never actually been to Sludgehaven, but he'd seen it on the map and it certainly wasn't just round the corner.

'Not the way I drive,' said TT. 'Once there, we make for the Ritz.' He sat back and waited for this to sink in.

'We're staying in the *Ritz*?' gasped O'Brian. The famous Ritz hotel! Imagine his brothers' faces! Whatever would they make of that?

'Yep,' said TT. 'Only the best for you boys.' He reached down, clicked open his briefcase and produced a glossy brochure. With a flourish, he threw it on the sticky table. 'There. Read all about it.'

The Boys stared at the brochure, which had a picture of the Ritz on the front. It certainly looked impressive.

'Five star,' said TT. 'Height of luxury. Feather beds. Gourmet food prepared by a top-class chef. A trouser press in every room. Every whim catered for. High-speed seagull service available on request.'

'What's that?' asked O'Brian.

'Like carrier pigeons, but with seagulls. So you'll be able to spend breakfast looking over your sacks of fan mail.'

'I doubt that,' said Arthur. He picked up the brochure and flicked through it, frowning. 'I don't think we have any actual fans.'

'Trust me. You will now you've hit the big time.'

'It's very expensive,' said Arthur. 'See this? Two hundred pounds a night. That's more than we get if we win.'

'*When* you win,' corrected TT. 'Anyway, that's just the start. We're getting a record contract, remember? We'll be millionaires in no time. Might as well start as we mean to continue. So we arrive at the Ritz, settle in, order up room service, start enjoying the Crash 'n' Bang lifestyle. Maybe throw a spellovision set out of the window.'

'We're going to throw a *spellovision set* out of the *window*?' gasped O'Brian.

'If we want to,' said TT. 'It's the sort of wild and crazy thing we do. We can wreck the place if we like.'

'Well, I don't think we should,' snapped Arthur.

'I'm just saying we *could*. Don't look like that – I'll pay for it.'

'How?' Arthur wanted to know. 'We're not millionaires yet. There's very little in the band kitty, you know.'

'Hey.' TT held up an admonishing finger. 'Leave all that to me, OK? I'm the manager now.'

'Then what?' begged O'Brian. 'Stop interrupting, Arthur. What next, TT?'

'An early night,' said TT firmly. 'We need to be up

bright and early next morning for the Battle. After breakfast, we drive to the field and find out from DJ Benny Bonkers what time you're on. He's the host for the day. Did I mention that?'

Everyone was impressed. DJ Benny Bonkers had his own show on the radio. It was called *Bonkers' Half Hour*.

'Then we find the hospitality tent,' went on TT. 'Grab a sandwich, meet the other bands. Talking of which . . .' He dived into his briefcase again and produced a sheet of paper. 'I've got a list. There's five.'

'Do we know any of them?'

'You tell me. There's a Skeleton outfit. *Rodney and the Rattles.*'

'Never heard of 'em,' said O'Brian.

'*One Big Troll and Some Other Biggish Ones?*'

'Nope.'

'*Betty and the Bully Girls? The Gnomettes?*'

Shrugs all round.

'Who's the fifth?' asked Filth.

'You. *The Witchway Rhythm Boys.*'

'Well, we've certainly got the best name,' said Arthur. Suddenly he felt excited. He very nearly Sparked Up, but managed to swallow it down. 'I reckon we'll wipe the floor with them.'

'You will,' agreed TT. 'You *will*. But there's just one little thing that's worrying me.'

'What's that?' enquired O'Brian.

'You need a singer,' said TT.

There was a little silence.

'I really don't think we *do*, you know,' said Arthur stiffly.

'Trust me,' said TT. 'Look, you boys can *play*, I know that. But none of you sing, right? If you had a singer who could put words to your wild and crazy tunes, it'd add a whole new dimension to the act. People like bands with singers. You need a front man. Someone to get the crowd going. Someone with fashionable trousers and a good hairdo. It's all to do with the image.'

'Thought it was all to do with the music,' muttered Filth.

'Trust me,' said TT again. 'The image is all-important. I'm the manager.'

'So you keep saying,' snapped Arthur.

'Well, I am. And let's face it, Arthur, you never got very far doing it your way, did you?'

'I did my best!' Arthur was getting cross now. 'Who are you to – to come marching in taking over! Cancelling our regular gigs and telling us what to do!'

'Well,' said TT, 'I'm sorry, but that's the way I operate. This is a *Battle*. We need all the weapons we can get. You want to win, don't you?'

'*Of course I want to win!*'

'Then get a singer. I'm telling you now, you won't stand a chance without one.'

At that moment, lunch arrived. Spag dumped the tray down on the table, slopping tea and spilling chips everywhere. Arthur hastily snatched up his folder and everyone mopped at their laps. O'Brian couldn't help noticing that he got the worst of it. His trousers were *soaked*.

'So,' went on TT, glaring at Spag's retreating back. 'We hold auditions tonight. I'll get posters put up in the Wood this afternoon. I've got some here.' He reached down to his briefcase, peeled it from the sticky floor, clicked it open and took out a pile of posters. 'What d'you think?'

He held one up. It said:

**CRASH 'N' BANG SINGER WONTID FOR UP-AND-CUMING BAND.
AWDISHUNS TONIT, SEVEN OCLOK, THE STOODY-O.**

'I don't believe this,' fumed Arthur. He appealed to O'Brian, who was bent over extracting soggy chips from his turn-ups. 'We don't want a singer, do we?'

'As your manager, I say you do,' said TT firmly. 'What do you think, Filth?'

'I dunno,' said Filth doubtfully. 'It's kinda late, dude.'

'No, it isn't,' said TT. 'Audition tonight, find a singer, practise with him tomorrow and off on Friday. Plenty of time. Right. On to the fan club. I've taken out an advertisement in tomorrow's *Miracle*. I'm expecting a big response. And I'm getting quotes in from doll companies. We'll need to take photographs so they can see what you look like.'

The Boys stared at him. Say what you like, this sounded like proper Management. Even Arthur was impressed. But – a *singer*?

'Oh, and last of all – the new look.' The Thing delved into the briefcase again and brought out a flat, floppy parcel wrapped in brown paper. He pulled off the string and the paper, revealing –

'Oh,' said Arthur. 'T-shirts. Right.'

'Great, aren't they?' enthused TT. 'I've brought a selection of colours. Purple, black and – a sort of – er – washed-out red. They're all one size, I'm afraid. But they're brand new. Well, two of them are. Help yourselves.'

Arthur took the purple one and held it up.

'It says "Moonmad" on it,' he said.

'Well, yes,' said TT. 'All the best ones do. Moonmad Management, that's me.'

'Shouldn't it be the band name, though?'

'Not necessarily. That's what everyone does. You'll be a bit different.'

Filth reached out and helped himself to the black one. O'Brian was too slow and ended up with the one at the bottom, which wasn't a sort of washed-out red at all.

'It's pink,' said O'Brian.

'Depends on the light,' said TT.

'No, it's pink. Wouldn't you call that pink?' O'Brian appealed to Filth, who agreed that it was.

'So what if it is?' said TT.

'I'm ginger, in case you hadn't noticed.'

'Make a change,' suggested TT. 'Just try it on – it might suit you.'

O'Brian poked at the material. It had a strange, almost rubbery texture, rather like a deflated balloon. It didn't feel nice.

'It's not exactly new either, is it?'

'No,' admitted TT. 'I didn't have any more new ones.'

This was actually a lie. He had plenty. But TT loved them all. He wasn't fond of purple and had more than one black, but he couldn't bring himself to part with any of the others. Luckily he had found the weird pink one jammed at the back of the bottom drawer. He hadn't a clue when it came from. He certainly didn't remember buying it. It seemed to have appeared from nowhere.

An enormous hairy paw plonked a bill on the table.

'Beel,' Conf growled. 'You pay now.'

'Right,' said TT and rummaged in his briefcase. He gave a little cry. 'Oh *no*! I've only gone and left my wallet at home. It'll have to be in change, I'm afraid.' He reached into his trouser pockets, then slapped his forehead. 'I don't *believe* it! I've filled my pockets with small pebbles instead! Easily done, I suppose.'

'Not *that* easily,' said Arthur.

'No, I'm always doing it,' explained TT, chuckling ruefully at his own silliness. 'When I clean out my goldfish, I wash the pebbles and pile them on the sideboard, you see, next to where I keep my spare change. Tell you what, if you all chip in a bit I'll refund you from petty cash once I've got the books sorted. Fair enough?'

It seemed fair enough. Grumbling a bit, the Boys finally managed to muster the required amount. Conf scooped it up and lumbered off.

'There you go,' said TT cheerily. 'Now you can tuck into the delicious lunch I've bought you.'

'You haven't actually b—' began Arthur, but was drowned out.

'A toast!' shouted TT, picking up a chipped, sticky mug full of orange tea. 'To the Battle of the Bands!'

'To the Battle of the Bands!' chorused everyone.

'To the contract!'

'To the contract!'

'To untold riches!'

'To untold riches!'

'To stardom and beyond!'

'To stardom and beyond!'

'To Crash 'n' Bang, man!' shouted Filth, eyes ablaze.

'To Crash 'n' Bang!' they all roared and O'Brian spilled his tea on purpose, just to show how dangerous he was.

It was all quite exciting!

Chapter Nine

Auditions

At seven o'clock on the dot, the Boys once again assembled at the Studio. TT (wearing another crisp new T-shirt in dazzling white) had set himself up at a small table just outside the door because there wasn't much room inside. As promised, he had put up posters all over the Wood and seemed confident that there would be a good response. The Boys weren't so sure.

They sat in silence, nervously eyeing the large X that the new manager had painted on the floor. All three were self-consciously wearing their new Moonmad T-shirts. Arthur's was on the short side. He'd had to cut holes in the back for his wings. His mum had hemmed them, but they still looked a bit odd. Still, at least it matched his scales. Filth's black one hung down past his knees. He thought he looked OK. O'Brian's weird pink one was, frankly, a disaster. He had unwisely tried it on over his jerkin and, much to his dismay, found he couldn't get it off again. It was painfully tight across his chest and bulged everywhere.

'It looks stupid, man,' Filth advised him.

'I know that,' said O'Brian irritably.

'So take it off.'

'D'you not think I've tried? It won't go over my ears. The neck's too small.'

'If it went on, it'll come off,' Arthur said.

But it wouldn't, even though they all gave a hand at tugging.

'I'll have to cut it off,' said O'Brian crossly. 'Leave me alone now, you're making me hot.'

Another little silence fell. From outside came the sound of TT shouting and bossing people about.

'I'm really not sure about this,' said Arthur. 'We've always managed without a singer before. It's all very well for him to talk, but he doesn't understand the *musical* problems. How's a singer supposed to learn our tunes in time for Saturday? And come up with words to put to them? It's ridiculous and I really think —'

He broke off as the new manager came scuttling in, armed with a clipboard.

'Right,' said TT, all efficiency. 'There's quite a queue outside, so we'd better kick off. First off, we've got a Gnome. Come in, young GNed, this is your big chance.'

A small Gnome trailed in, looking horribly nervous. Or gnervous.

'I'll leave you to it,' said TT. 'Three minutes, that's all you've got.' And he bustled out. The Gnome stared down at the floor, clearly hoping it would open up and swallow him.

'Hello, GNed,' said Arthur, taking pity. 'Stand on the X, if you please. Don't be scared – we won't bite. What are you going to sing for us today?'

GNed fished in his pocket and withdrew a crumpled piece of paper.

'Song,' he mumbled.

'Good,' said Arthur kindly. 'And what is it called, this song?'

' "Tra la la".'

'Well, when you're ready.'

Puce in the face, GNed cleared his throat.

'*Tra la la*,' he muttered. '*Tra la la la la la la la la la la la la . . .*'

'Oh, man,' sighed Filth.

'Thank you, GNed,' interrupted Arthur. 'I think we've got the hang of the lyrics. Perhaps you'd like to sing us the tune?'

'I just did,' said GNed.

And that was the beginning.

GNed was followed by a Dwarf with an axe who attempted the traditional 'Hi-Ho' song. Unlike 'Tra la la', it had proper words, but the Dwarf had a voice like a crow with croup and dropped his aitches, which didn't help with all those 'hi's and 'ho's going on. Even worse, he added actions – chopping motions with the axe and so on. Not only was he bad, he was seriously dangerous.

Next up was a foul-tempered Tree Demon who instantly blotted his copybook by refusing to stand on the X. He said he'd stand wherever he blinkin' well liked – who were they to tell him what to do? When Arthur insisted, he kicked over Filth's side drum and stormed out, taking his song with him. So that was a waste of time. Even if he'd been any good, they couldn't take the attitude.

The Tree Demon was followed by three gum-chewing teenage Banshees, their hair wildly back-combed and their nightgowns ripped in a fashionable teenage way. They sidled through the door, whispering and pushing each other, saying, 'Go on, ask him.'

'Ask me what?' said Arthur tiredly.

'Can we have his autograph?' said the tallest, pointing at Filth, who was off in Drum World, tapping out little rhythms on his side drum.

'No,' said Arthur shortly. 'You can't. Not now.'

'You can have mine,' offered O'Brian shyly.

'No,' said the Banshee. 'Just his.'

'This is a singing audition,' said Arthur sternly. 'Are you girls here to sing?'

'No. Just the autograph. He's to make it out to Charlene.'

'And Jemella,' said the second.

'And Roxanne,' said the third.

'It's not a good time,' insisted Arthur.

All three Banshees folded their arms and looked mutinous. TT came marching in.

'All right, girls, move along. You have to go through the proper channels. There's a fan club you can join. All the autographs you like, together with a signed photo. Very reasonable rates. Details in tomorrow's *Miracle*.'

'Who are you, bossin' us around?' sniffed Charlene.

'I'm the manager. Off you go now, the Boys are busy.'

'We don't want *him* in the photo,' said Jemella, pointing at Arthur.

'Or him,' said Roxanne, giving O'Brian an unkind sneer.

The three of them trailed out, looking disappointed and craning their necks to look back at Filth, who didn't even notice.

'All right, you can send in the next one,' said Arthur to TT, rather crossly.

'Actually,' said TT, 'that's it. There aren't any more.'

'I thought you said there was a long queue,' wheezed O'Brian from the constrictions of his T-shirt.

'There was, but they've all gone home. There's Goblin Football on the spellovision and it's chilly out there.'

'So that's it, then,' said Arthur, trying not to sound too relieved. 'Interesting idea, but it seems we'll have to carry on as we . . .'

'Um – excuse me?' said a voice. Everyone looked round – and stared. Peering through the doorway was . . .

A Werewolf!

In a frock!

Chapter Ten

Tallula

There was deathly silence. Even Filth stopped tapping and came back to earth. Werewolves were seldom seen down in the Wood. They tend to be solitary, antisocial types who live alone in remote mountain caves. Little was known about them. They were a bit of a mystery, particularly the girls.

Everyone's eyes slowly travelled from the Werewolf's huge feet up, up, up to the top of her head. She was *tall*.

She was also covered from head to foot in thick brown hair. It rippled when she moved. It grew on her arms. It grew on her legs. It grew on the backs of her hands. Most of it sprouted from her head in a thick mane. She had scraped some of it back into a messy ponytail, tied with a bit of old twine. The rest hung down in a curtain over her eyes.

The frock was – well, horrible. A sort of washed-out, shapeless sack with an uneven hem that sagged round her knees.

'Yes?' said TT. 'Can I help you?'

'Am I too late?' asked the Werewolf girl.

'To – *sing*, you mean?' asked TT with a frown.

'Yes.' The Werewolf girl ducked under the low doorway and stepped into the Studio, which immediately seemed much smaller.

'Ah,' said TT. 'Now, there's a bit of a problem. This is actually a *Boy* Band, you see. The clue's in the name.'

'It didn't say boys only on the poster,' said the Werewolf girl.

'It should have,' said TT. 'I was in a bit of a hurry. This is Crash 'n' Bang music, you see. Manly sort of stuff.'

'Are you saying girls can't like Crash 'n'Bang?'

'You can *like* it,' said TT. 'In fact, I'm setting up a fan club you can join –'

'But we can't sing it?' interrupted the Werewolf girl. 'There's some sort of rule? Is that what you're saying?'

'What I'm saying,' said TT, 'what I'm *saying* is,

you couldn't call it *The Witchway Rhythm Boys and a Werewolf Girl*. It'd look silly on the posters.'

'So I can't audition, then?'

'W-e-e-e-ll . . . How can I put this? No.'

There was an awkward little pause. And then, to everyone's surprise, Filth suddenly said, 'Hey, man. Why not?'

TT could think of plenty more reasons why not, apart from the whole girl thing. He began with the next big one that came to mind, which was the whole Werewolf thing.

'Look,' he said. 'Let's not beat about the bush. Don't you lot go funny at full moon?'

Filth, Arthur and O'Brian glanced at each other uncomfortably. The question seemed a bit personal. Still, it would be good to know.

'Funny?' The Werewolf girl stared at him.

'Yes,' said TT sternly. '*Funny*. You know. Run around gnashing your teeth and howling.'

'Well, I usually stay in and make biscuits.'

In the background, Filth gave a little snigger.

'There's more to us than charging around drooling, you know,' went on the Werewolf girl. 'We do have *lives*.'

'All right, keep your hair on,' said TT.

'Anyway,' said the Werewolf girl, 'what about you? You wear a T-shirt with Moonmad on it.'

'Doesn't mean I am, though.'

'Well, neither am I. But even if I was, what's that got to do with singing?'

'Nothing,' said Filth. 'Let her try, man – she's here now.'

'Quite right,' said Arthur, forcing a smile on to his lips. He liked to think of himself as fair. After all, it wasn't her fault she looked like – well, like *that*.

'To be sure, give the lass a go,' said O'Brian, who was feeling a bit faint and just wanted to get the whole thing over with. Go home, find some scissors and liberate himself from T-shirt prison. He added, 'Make it quick, eh?'

TT gave in. He picked up his clipboard with a little sigh.

'Name?'

'Tallula. T-A-L-L-U-L-A.'

TT wrote it down.

'I suppose you're called that because you're –'

'Tall? No. It's my name. Is it a problem?'

'Oh, no, no. It's quite a nice name, actually. Not at all wolfish. I expect people are surprised when they –'

'See me in the flesh? Yes. They are.'

'Right,' said TT. 'Well, stand on the X, er – Tallula. I take it you've got something prepared?'

Tallula nodded. All eyes were on her as she stepped carefully on the white cross, then reached into the pocket of her frock and produced a little black book.

'I've got some lyrics here,' she said shyly. 'I thought they might go with that new number you were playing the other night? With the extra-long drum solo? Where you double up the tempo at the end?'

The Boys looked at each other, startled.

'You heard that?' asked O'Brian.

'Yes.' Tallula blushed a bit beneath her hair. 'I was outside, under the willow tree. I'm there most nights. Whenever you rehearse.'

'Er – why?' enquired Arthur.

'I like hearing you play, that's all,' said Tallula, her eyes sliding sideways to Filth.

'Oh. Really? Well. That's good,' said Arthur. 'So – fire away, then. Let's hear it.'

Tallula straightened her shoulders, drew herself up to her considerable full height, took a deep breath, threw back her head, opened her mouth – and sang!

> '*I used to be a loner,*
> *I used to be a freak,*
> *I used to be a moaner,*
> *I used to be a geek,*

But since I started singing,
My life has changed and how!
I used to be a Werewolf but I'm all right now.
I'm all right noooooooow!
Yes, I'm all right noooooooow!
I can growl, I can bite,
But I can sing, so that's all right,
Used to be a Werewolf but I'm
A-l-l-l-l-l-lll
Ri-i-i-i-ght
NOOOOOOOOOOWWWWWW!

The final howl died away. It was spine-chilling. But in a sort of *good* way.

There was a long silence. Nobody spoke. Nobody moved.

'That's it,' said Tallula. 'What do you think?' The Boys and TT were staring at her, open-mouthed. 'Too wolfish for you? Well, thanks anyway . . .'

She closed her little black book, slipped it in her pocket and turned to leave. Her shoulders had slumped back down again. And then —

'Wait,' said Filth. He picked up his drumstick. His eyes were shining.

'What key are you in?' said Arthur, turning to the piano. 'F, wasn't it?'

'Sing the opening again, would you?' said O'Brian, raising his whistle to his lips.

And Tallula belted out the opening again.

'I used to be a loner,
I used to be a freak . . .'

And the Boys joined in. Drums crashed, the piano leapt into life and the penny whistle added perfect little toodles in all the right places. It was loud. It was strong. It worked! As for that voice . . .

TT threw his clipboard to one side and leaned against the shed wall with his arms folded. His foot was tapping and he was grinning broadly.

He thought it unlikely that she possessed a pair of fashionable trousers. And there was no way he would find a T-shirt to fit her. But there was no doubt about it.

Tallula was fantastic!

Chapter Eleven

Two Meetings

Scott Sinister, famous star of stage and screen, lounged on his sumptuous sofa staring at the Genie who sat in the armchair opposite, smiling toothily.

A visit from any old Genie would be an event. But this wasn't any old Genie. This was none other than Ali Pali. *The* Ali Pali. The Genie with the golden touch. The rich, successful entrepreneur Genie who owned Witchway Spellovision and lived a life of enviable luxury in a marble palace with sherbet fountains and a heated swimming pool. The sort of Genie you wanted to keep *in* with.

'Mystery Celebrity, eh?' mused Scott. 'A Battle of the Bands. Hmm. I must admit it sounds intriguing.'

'Excellent!' cried Ali, beaming away like a beacon. 'I knew I could count on you!'

Like all Genies, Ali was a flashy dresser. On his head was the traditional bejewelled turban. On his feet were the curly-toed slippers. He went in for a lot of glittery jewellery. He had, however, wisely exchanged the traditional skimpy bolero and flimsy pants combination for an expensive-looking golden business suit, cut cleverly to hide his tummy.

At his feet was the shabby old carpet bag he always carried to remind himself of his humble roots (he used to sell flying carpets). Scott knew all about Ali's bag because it had featured in a celebrity magazine called *Famous and Fabulous*. The magazine ran a regular article called *What's In Their Bags?* Ali's bag contained all his mystical Genie stuff — magical gifts, purses of gold, priceless jewels, a packet of sherbet lemons and spare golden underwear.

'Mind you,' went on Scott, 'I'll have to consult my diary. I'm greatly in demand for public appearances. My latest film has received rave reviews.'

This was true. Scott's career was currently at an all-time high. His personal life was good too, now that his ex-girlfriend had finally stopped sending him poison pen letters.

'Ah.' Ali nodded sympathetically. 'It is the price of fame.'

'You've *seen* my latest film, I take it?'

'*Avenging Killer Poodles – The Final Chapter!*' Ali clasped his plump hands together. 'A masterpiece! Your greatest work. Three times I have been. Wonderful!'

He hadn't seen it at all, actually. He was too busy making money to go to the cinema. But Ali knew how to flatter celebrities.

'I have the reviews here somewhere.' Scott dug into the pocket of his silken dressing gown. 'You might like to . . . ?'

'Sadly, I have no time.' Ali sounded wretched. 'Places to fly, people to see, you know how it is.'

'Oh. Well, the critics love it. Mind you, making it left me quite, quite exhausted. Never act with animals, Mr Pali. Those poodles were *savages*.'

'Tch, tch,' tutted Ali. 'What it is to suffer for the art. What you need is a day in the glorious sunshine.'

'Hmm. Sludgehaven, you say? Why there, particularly?'

'It is the only place with a big enough field,' explained Ali. 'We are expecting great crowds, you see.'

Scott thought about this. He had mixed memories of Sludgehaven. He had performed there once at the Pier Pavilion for a summer season. It had been the scene of one of his greatest triumphs. He wouldn't mind revisiting it, for old times' sake. But he didn't want to seem too easy.

'It's hardly just round the corner, is it? How am I supposed to get there?'

'I will send a limousine,' Ali informed him smoothly. 'Also, I have taken the liberty of booking you into the luxurious Ritz hotel. Arrive Friday, stay overnight, linger over the delicious breakfast in the morning, then be driven in style to the hospitality tent.'

'A private one, I hope?' put in Scott. 'I hope I'm not expected to mix with the bands.'

'Why, of course not! You are the star of stage and screen! There will be a special celebrity tent where you will recline on the shiny cushions eating grapes. Then a little light judging, sign a few autographs, pose with a few fans, large cheque in the post. What could be easier?'

'Will it be spellovised?' enquired Scott. Although principally a star of stage and the big screen, Scott loved seeing himself on spellovision.

'Of course,' said Ali. 'This is the big day! The launch of *Genie Sounds*. It will be on prime time. And the press will be out in force. The *Sludgehaven News*. *The Daily Miracle*. *Famous and Fabulous* have promised to send along their top reporter.'

'Well,' said Scott, 'as it happens, I think I *am* free on Saturday.'

'A thousand rejoicings!' Ali clapped his hands. 'My work is done!'

'Who else is on the judging panel?' enquired Scott. 'As well as me.'

'Well, my humble self, of course. And the Mayor of Sludgehaven.'

'Hardly a celebrity,' scoffed Scott.

'No,' admitted Ali, 'but it was the only way I could persuade him to hire out the field. He is afraid of hordes of music fans running amok in the streets of Sludgehaven, frightening the little children and kicking in the windows of the cream tea shops.' Ali gave a little sigh, then brightened. 'But no matter! I am in negotiations with another *proper* celebrity.'

'Who?' asked Scott sharply. 'Not as famous as me, surely?'

'No, no!' cried Ali. 'You are my shining star!'

'Who, then?'

'Ah.' Ali tapped the side of his nose. 'Big secret until all is confirmed. But rest assured you are the tops. And now, allow me to present you with the traditional gifts. It is the Genie way.'

He dived into the carpet bag, re-emerging with a small box of Turkish delight adorned with a red ribbon. This was followed by a sequinned belt, a small rubber camel that squirted water when you squeezed its hump, a bar of sandalwood soap, a plastic palm tree and a signed photograph of Ali himself, reclining on a bed of cushions next to his heated swimming pool.

It was an odd collection, and frankly a bit disappointing after all that talk of purses of gold.

'You like?' beamed Ali.

'Er – well, um, yes. Thanks very much.'

'It is my pleasure.' Ali Pali stood up. 'And now I must leave you. There is much to organise.'

'Shall the butler order you a cab?'

'No. I flew in. My carpet awaits. Farewell, my friend. I shall be in touch.'

Luscious Lulu Lamarre, star of stage and screen, sat at her dressing-room mirror, which was surrounded by twinkling lights. She wore a satin evening dress. Diamonds glittered at her neck. She was busily powdering her nose, getting ready for the matinee performance. From somewhere outside came the sound of the orchestra tuning up.

Life was good for Lulu. She was currently starring in a musical show entitled *Singalongalulu!* It was very popular with a certain weird section of the public. Every night was booked out. Fans queued at the stage door, their arms full of flowers, cards and chocolates. Even better, she had stopped writing poison pen letters to her ex-boyfriend and moved on. Yes, everything was good. Although she would have preferred it if her visitor had arrived *after* the performance. Lulu liked to allow plenty of time to pout at her reflection and plump up her hair before making her grand entrance.

The visitor sat beaming away in the background, plump little hands folded across his belly and carpet bag at his feet.

Lulu knew Ali Pali. He had once been her manager. Quite a good one, as it happened. They had both since moved on to other things, but she had to admit that he had done wonders for her career.*

'So, Lulu, my darling,' said Ali. 'Will you do it? What do you say?'

'I don't *know*.' Lulu gave a petulant little wriggle of her shoulders. 'It's very short notice, Ali.'

'Ah, come on. For Ali, eh? Remember Sludgehaven?

---

* Read all about it in *Pongwiffy and the Holiday of Doom*.

The summer season at the Pier Pavilion? Back in the old days?'

'I most certainly do.' Lulu gave a little shudder. 'But that's all behind me. I'm a household name now.'

'Exactly! All the households will be tuning in to see their favourite star on the spellovision. My top cameraman will be there. You will get all the big, lingering close-ups, I promise.'

'But what about the show? I'm the star! You've seen it, I hope?'

'I have,' lied Ali. 'Three times I have been. You were wonderful.'

'I know. That's what I'm saying. It's always a full house on Saturdays. My public needs me.'

'Send on the understudy,' said Ali.

'But it's called *Singalongalulu!*'

'Call it *Singalongatheunderstudy!* It's only for one night.' Ali was really wheedling now. 'Darling. Sweetie. Help me out here. I really need you for this. I need glamour on the panel. Who is more glamorous than Luscious Lulu Lamarre?'

'True,' agreed Lulu. 'I suppose you're right. I take it there's a fee?'

'Of course. A most *generous* fee. I shall send a limousine for you, and I have booked you into the Ritz, of course. It will be a day of glorious sunshine and music. You will sit and smile for the camera and give everyone the benefit of your beauty and wisdom. Ah, say you will, darling. Be a Mystery Celebrity for Ali. Eh?'

'W-e-e-l-l . . . Who else is on the panel?'

'My humble self and the Mayor of Sludgehaven.'

'Poo!' Lulu gave a little pout. 'You and some boring old Mayor. Is that all?'

'Not quite. I am in negotiations with someone else.'

'Who?'

'Ah.' Ali tapped his nose. 'For now, big secret. Someone famous.'

'Not as famous as me, though?'

'No, no! You are my shining star!'

'Well – all right, then. I suppose I'll do it.'

'A thousand rejoicings! Allow me to present you with the traditional gifts!'

'Are they the same ones you always hand out? The Turkish delight and the soap and the cheap belt and the photo of you in your trunks?'

'Yes.'

'No, then.'

'Not the amusing rubber camel that squirts the water when the hump is squeezed?'

'No. I've already got one.'

'Ah, well. It is your choice.' Ali Pali stood up. 'I shall leave you to prepare. I have another appointment. I must fly. Wonderful to see you, darling. I shall be in touch.'

Chapter Twelve

Setting Off

'Yeee-haaaaa!' shouted TT, twirling the wheel deftly as the band van charged along the track. 'See that, Gareth? See how I missed that tree? Woo-hooo!'

It was early Friday morning, and TT was in a terrific mood. He had finally found his calling! His life was back on track! He was the manager of an up-and-coming band with an amazing new singer and was off to Sludgehaven-on-Sea! Gareth was coming too in his bowl, which was firmly sticky-taped to the dashboard. He looked quite excited, for a fish.

TT had acquired the van the day before. It had been the first job on his list of things to do. The list went like this:

1. Get a van (how?)

2. Get some munny (how?)

3. Buy sum stuff (how?)

4. Get a roadie (who?)

5. Pak T-shirts

6. Pak Gareth's fude

7. Pak Gareth

8. Arange for fan mail to be sent to hotel

9. Book hotel

There was a lot to organise, but TT thrived on being busy. The Boys were tied up with rehearsing the new singer, so TT had left them to it and set off to pay a visit to Helpful Bob.

Helpful Bob was the owner of a recently opened Emporium called Essential Necessities, which basically sold anything people thought they wanted. Bob's big selling point was that there was no money down. You just took the goods and paid later, which didn't hurt so much at the time, although later it hurt a *lot*. TT had worked briefly for Bob once. For one long, boring night, he had attempted to hand out Bob's advertising fliers. After failing to shift more than one – and that to a stupid Goblin which ended up causing a lot of trouble – long story – TT had got fed up, dumped the fliers and gone home.*

To his relief, Bob didn't bear a grudge. He said he quite understood about the fliers, always difficult to shift, all water under the bridge, etc., etc. He smiled and nodded and treated TT like a valued customer. What did sir require? A band van? Of course. What were sir's exact requirements? How many seats? What colour? Anything written on the side? Brand new and flashy or old and funky, with a history? Fluffy dice? Radio? Roof rack, perhaps? No problem, sir was in luck, there was one just like it in the warehouse. If sir would just excuse him, he'd drive it round. Back in two shakes.

TT couldn't believe his eyes when he saw it. The van was GREAT! It was old and beat-up, like a proper band van should be. It had six seats at the front and plenty of space at the back for the equipment. The

* For more details, read *Pongwiffy and the Important Announcement*.

94

outside was painted a dirty black with huge red letters rising dramatically out of orange flames. The letters screamed:

**THE WITCHWAY RHYTHM BOYS –
THE TOUR!
ORGANISED BY MOONMAD
MANAGEMENT**

It had a roof rack. The number plate read RBOYZ 1. The exhaust pipe was hanging off in time-honoured band van fashion. Most of the lights were on the blink. There were fluffy dice. There was a radio. It was just the right combination of flashy and grotty. It was utterly perfect.

'No money down, you say?' asked TT.

'Why, no!' cried Bob, shocked.

'I'll take it,' said TT happily. 'Er – and while I'm about it, I'm after a few other things. I'm going on a trip, you see. I've just started managing an up-and-coming Crash 'n' Bang band and we're entering for a competition and about to become millionaires.'

'Is that so? Well, congratulations, sir. I'm sure you'll make a go of it.'

'Thanks. I'm keen to do it in style.'

'That's the only way,' agreed Helpful Bob. 'Top-rate

hotel. Money no object. Little luxuries. Slap-up meals. You only live once, eh?'

'Absolutely!' cried TT. 'Trouble is, although I'll soon be a millionaire, I'm a bit short of cash right now.'

'Ah,' said Helpful Bob. He reached under the counter and brought out a small rectangular card. It was gold coloured. It caught the light. 'Now, I wonder if you've seen one of these? I only offer them to valued customers. I call it a Magic Card.'

Bob explained all about the Magic Card. Apparently, you could buy what you liked with no actual money changing hands. This was great, because TT didn't have any actual money. A Magic Card was exactly what he needed.

As soon as it was in his hot little hand, TT used it to buy a few other things as well. Driving gloves. A camera. A gold watch. A baseball cap with MANAGER written on it. It was all good, but the van was the best. He drove it home, singing all the way. He spent the rest of the day working through the other items on his list – packing T-shirts and hunting for sticky tape to attach Gareth's bowl to the dashboard and so on – but kept breaking off to run outside and admire the van, which was without doubt the most exciting thing he had ever purchased.

And now it was the following day and he was off to show it to the Boys. But first, he had a mystery passenger to pick up. That'd be another surprise for them! Then in no time at all he'd be out of the Wood and joining the main road to Sludgehaven, where the Boys would be waiting. And the new singer, hopefully. TT was looking forward to hearing how she was getting on. Shame about the hair, of course – and the frock, and the whole Werewolf girl thing – but the voice made up for her deficiencies in the image department.

'Woo-hoo!' shouted TT again, as a wheel went down a pothole and the van lurched, causing a small tidal wave in Gareth's bowl. 'Sludgehaven, here we come!'

'Oh my!' gasped Sludgegooey as the van came hurtling round the corner in a cloud of grey smoke and drew up alongside in a cacophony of honking horn and squealing brakes. There came a series of loud bangs from the exhaust pipe as the engine revved and roared. 'What in the world is that?' She clutched Filth's arm and pointed theatrically.

'Wow!' said Filth. 'The band van, man! That is something *else*!'

'No, it's definitely a van,' said Sludgegooey.

The pair of them stood on the grass verge beside the road, surrounded by Filth's boxed-up drums. That was his only luggage apart from a small back-pack containing a couple of cheese sandwiches, a comb, a toothbrush, a bottle of black nail polish and a jar of hair gel.

Sludgegooey had got up especially early to see Filth off. She had even made his sandwiches. In addition, she had made a small cardboard sign with the words GUD LUK BOYS which was pleasantly supportive. Of course, she was mostly in it for the money, but nobody could accuse her of not doing her bit.

Mind you, she hoped the whole departure business wouldn't take too long. She was getting particularly fed up with three teenage Banshees who had sud-denly appeared and were hanging around in the background, whispering and chewing and rolling their eyes at Filth. Charlene, Jemella and Roxanne had got wind of the Boys' early departure and come to wave them off. They had a big banner with them. It said WE LUV U FILTH. It had red hearts on, and glitter. Sludgegooey felt her own sign was being upstaged.

Standing alongside Filth and Sludgegooey was Arthur with his piano parked on its cart, all wrapped up in its blanket. He had a small suitcase in his hand

and his mother was leaning on his arm. This is the first time we've seen Arthur's mother. She looks like an older, more wrinkly female version of Arthur, with the addition of a skirt and a walking stick. She had got up to make sandwiches too – mustard ones with the crusts cut off, just how Arthur liked them. She had also provided him with extra-strong pepper-mints in case he couldn't buy the ones he liked on the road, together with lots of useful paper hankies in case he needed to clean anything. She was very thoughtful, was Arthur's mother.

She squinted up at the smoking, pulsating monster filling her vision.

'Very nice, son,' she said. 'Very – what's that phrase you use? To describe your lovely music?'

'Crash 'n' Bang, Mam,' said Arthur. 'It's definitely Crash 'n' Bang, that van.'

The driver's door opened and TT scrambled out.

'What d'you think?' he demanded. 'Said there'd be a van, didn't I? Six-seater. Like the colour? See the writing on the side? The dice? It's even got a radio!'

'A radio?' Filth nearly fainted with joy. 'Cool! Does it work?'

'No,' admitted TT. 'I don't think so. But it's got one. Wait, there's more.' He scuttled to the back and flung open the double doors. 'See? Plenty of room for the instruments.'

Even Arthur had to admit that the van was good. The new manager was really delivering. Even if he was a bit pushy. The cap with MANAGER on it was a bit too much, in Arthur's opinion.

'O'Brian's late.' TT glanced sternly at his new watch. Arthur wondered where he had got it. He hadn't had it on the last time. 'I need him here now for the photograph. I'll get the camera. Did I mention the camera? State-of-the-art – comes with a tripod and cloth and everything. Bought it with the Magic Card.'

'The what?' said Arthur.

'I've got a Magic Card. Didn't I tell you? It's a new thing – all band managers have 'em. Saves messing about with money.' TT reached into the van for the camera. 'I need to take a photo for the fan club. The Boys And Their Supporters Getting Ready To Depart. Right, girls?' He raised an eyebrow at the Banshees, who squealed excitedly and began fussing with their hair. 'I'll set it up and the roadie can start loading.'

'The *what?*' chorused Filth and Arthur together.

'Ah. Didn't mention that, did I? Another little surprise for you.' TT put his fingers in his mouth and blew a shrill whistle.

The passenger door opened and a squat figure thumped down into the road and stood grinning at them.

'Chip?' said Arthur.

'Uh,' said Chip the Troll. He had dispensed with his apron and the rubber gloves. He now wore a straining Moonmad T-shirt in a dirty shade of plum – clearly one of the bottom-drawer variety – and had cut the sleeves off in order to better display the glory of his bulging biceps.

'I headhunted him,' explained TT cheerfully. 'Got the idea when I saw him with those potato sacks. Strong boy, he is. We need someone to handle the equipment. He's exploited in that cafe. He's always wanted to be a roadie and go on tour. Isn't that right, Chip?'

'Uh,' said Chip happily.

'What – he actually *said* that?' asked Arthur.

'Well – no. But I put it to him and he grunted and it definitely meant yes. Take it away, Chip!'

Chip was a Troll of few words – well, one, actually – but much action. He spat on his hands, hoisted Arthur's piano on to his back, cart and all, and heaved it into the van. Arthur winced as it crashed down. Then Chip began picking up Filth's beloved drums and hurling them in alongside. He was enthusiastic, but not especially careful.

'Hey, man!' protested Filth. 'Show some respect, yeah?'

The air wobbled and O'Brian was suddenly amongst them. In his arms was a large, grubby, round earthenware pot. Another of his fingers was bandaged, there was a hole in the knee of his jolly red trousers and he was still wearing the awful, constricting pink T-shirt over his jerkin. He looked a bit fed up.

'Sorry,' he sighed. 'Took a while to dig this up. Then I tried to dismantle the Rainbow Deflector and store it inside. But I had to leave it up in the end.'

'Why?' enquired Arthur.

'I fell off the roof,' admitted O'Brian.

He had too. Yet one more thing to add to his spate of bad luck, which he had initially put down to coincidence. Was it, though? Nothing had gone right ever since – well, ever since the business with the Fairy. He had a bad feeling that he might have been a bit hasty there.

'That's the secret pot of gold, I take it?' asked Arthur, staring at the earthenware pot which still had clods of earth clinging to it.

'Yes,' said O'Brian. 'This is the Pot.'

'Very nice,' said Arthur's mum kindly. She gave

Sludgegooey a little nudge. 'It's a very *nice* pot, don't you think?'

'Bit of a let-down, I'd say,' said Sludgegooey, who believed in being frank. 'Not at all what I imagined. All those Leprechaun stories about rainbows and stuff. I thought it'd be more impressive. Not just a big, dirty old pot.'

'It's dirty because I've just dug it up,' said O'Brian defensively. 'And it needs to be big because there's a lot of gold in it.'

'Let's see,' said Sludgegooey.

'I never *open* it,' explained O'Brian. 'I just have it.'

'Ridiculous,' scoffed Sludgegooey. 'Having a pot of gold and not even opening it. You Leprechauns are mad.'

'Well, anyway, it's very nice,' said Arthur's mother.

'It's a liability,' said Arthur sternly. 'I thought we'd agreed to travel light. What do you want to bring that for?'

'Because someone might steal it while I'm gone.'

'Clever!' howled Sludgegooey. 'He's scared someone'll pinch it so he's taking it to a crowded music festival where everyone *knows* you don't get thieves. What a genius!'

'They can't pinch it if I'm holding it,' said O'Brian. He clutched the Pot tightly to his chest. 'I'd see them do it and run after them.'

'Ah, but you'll have to put it down sometime. And the second you do, mark my words, it'll get stolen.'

'Look,' said O'Brian. 'Look, just stop picking on me, will you? I can look after my own Pot. *What?*'

Filth was beckoning him over for a private word.

'The T-shirt over the jerkin,' said Filth quietly. 'Not a good look, man.'

'I know,' said O'Brian. 'I *know*, all right?'

'So do something, dude.'

'I've *tried*. I nearly strangled myself trying to get it off last night.'

'Thought you were going to cut it off?'

'I was, but there's something odd about the material. The scissors won't go through. Or the leather knives, or the shears. I hacked away for hours, but all the tools went blunt.'

'Well, there's gotta be a reason. Hey! TT!' Filth raised his voice. 'Like, what's with O'Brian's T-shirt, man? He still can't get it off. Dude's stuck in it.'

TT shrugged, clearly uninterested. He had the new camera mounted on its tripod and was shaking out the cloth.

'I'm just thinking,' mumbled O'Brian, trying to sound casual, 'just wondering if there might be – I don't know, I know it sounds weird, but it's almost like there might be some sort of – um – *curse* on it. Or something.'

'Rubbish,' snorted Sludgegooey, who had sidled up and was listening. She considered herself an expert on such matters. 'A curse on a T-shirt! I've never heard of such a thing.'

'Whoever would put a curse on a T-shirt, O'Brian?' agreed Arthur. 'You haven't upset any Witches or anything, have you?'

'We'd do more than curse his T-shirt,' said Sludgegooey.

O'Brian bit his lip. He had already said too much. Confessing that he'd lost the goodwill of the Fairies was hardly likely to endear him to the present company. Right now, they needed all the luck they could get.

There came the sound of the van doors slamming. Chip had finished the loading.

'Where's the We— Tallula?' asked TT.

'We're picking her up in the mountains,' explained Arthur. 'That's where her cave is. She said she wanted to wash her hair. That takes a while, apparently. There's rather a lot of it.'

'I do like a nice head of hair,' said Arthur's mum happily.

'Ye-e-e-e-s,' said Arthur. 'Not all of it's on her head, of course. But she can certainly sing,' he added hastily. 'That's what really matters.'

'How did the rehearsals go?' asked TT, ducking under the cloth. 'She do all right?'

'Oh yes,' said Arthur. 'She did better than all right.'

And she had. She had done better than any of them could imagine. Tallula was a natural. Not only did she know all their old Crash 'n' Bang tunes, she had ideas for new ones. Her little black book was bursting with good words for songs. The minute she started humming, you just *knew* how it should go. Everything fitted together like a dream. The time had flashed by. The Boys had never enjoyed rehearsing so much.

'Good,' said TT. 'Well, she won't be in the photograph, but that's probably no bad thing. Chip, get Gareth from the dashboard. I want him in this too. Everybody close up together in front of the van. Band and supporters. Big smiles.'

'I won't have my photo taken right now, if you don't mind,' said O'Brian. He knew he didn't look his best. Besides, he was the only one who didn't have any supporters to wave him off. That made him feel a bit left out.

He climbed in the van and settled himself down with the Pot cradled on his lap while everyone else had their picture taken.

'That's it!' cried TT. He handed the camera to Chip, who threw it in the back of the van, breaking one of the tripod legs. 'Let's hit the road!'

'Thank goodness for that,' said Sludgegooey, relieved. 'Off you go, then, Filth. See you Sunday, with the cheque.'

'Good luck, son,' said Arthur's mum and gave him a motherly hug.

TT climbed into the driver's seat. Carefully, he re-stuck Gareth's bowl on the dashboard and started the engine. Filth squeezed in beside O'Brian. Arthur and Chip took the seats behind.

'What's with the fish, man?' enquired Filth. 'I gotta ask. Is it, like, a mascot?'

'Oh, Gareth is much more than that,' said TT. 'My Aunty Maureen gave him to me. He's family.'

'Ridiculous idea,' snorted Arthur. 'Bringing a gold-fish on tour.'

'Just because he's a fish it doesn't mean he can't have opinions,' said TT. 'I talk to him all the time. He's a very good listener. Very wise, actually.'

'You're saying it's – what, some sort of fish *oracle*?' sneered Arthur.

'Believe me, fish are deep. There's more to Gareth than you think.'

'Rubbish,' said Arthur.

'Well, you don't have to believe me,' said TT, 'but don't call him *it* – he doesn't like it. Right, everybody, seat belts on!'

The engine revved – Arthur's mother waved a handkerchief – Sludgegooey held up her GUD LUK sign. The Banshees produced colourful pompoms, brandished their banner and began chanting a little cheerleader ditty they'd composed. It went:

> *'Off on tour so toodle-ooo!*
> *Good luck, Filth, 'cos we love you!'*

Filth didn't notice because he was fiddling with the knobs on the radio.

And they were off!

Chapter Thirteen

In the Van

Tallula stood in the shadow of a tall tree, waiting to be picked up. The day was warming up
and she wasn't a great one for sunshine, which made
her hair greasy. She had washed it the night before,
using a whole family-sized bottle of shampoo. She
wondered if anyone would notice the difference.
Probably not.

At her feet was a small suitcase. She had packed
and repacked it three times, although there wasn't
much to put in. She had no clothes apart from her
frock, which she had never liked but always wore
because she hated shopping. She had put in her
hairbrush, her toothbrush, her little black book, her
pencil and a paper bag full of moon-shaped biscuits.
She intended to hand them round during the journey.

Tallula hardly ever left her cave in daylight, let alone set off on a trip which would involve singing in public in a big field in faraway Sludgehaven, which she had never visited. Werewolves aren't great ones for the seaside. When they do go on holiday – a rare event – they spend most of the time trying to come up with the name of a friend to send a postcard to. Tallula wondered about sending a card to her friend Shirley, who she hadn't seen since they had fallen out over a hairbrush when they were six. Then she remembered that she didn't have an address.

There came the sound of a blaring horn and the band van came screaming up the track in a cloud of dust. Tallula took a deep breath, stepped out into the sunshine and gave a wave.

The van squealed to a halt. The window rolled down and TT's head popped out.

'Hop in!' he shouted.

'Right!' called Tallula. 'Er – where?'

There was only one seat spare but she saw at once that there wasn't room for her long limbs.

'It'll have to be in the back, with the instruments.'

'Oh. Right.'

Tallula walked round to the back and wrenched open the doors. The back was pretty much filled with equipment, but there was a dark space between the

piano and drums into which she could just about squeeze, if she folded her knees and kept her head down.

'Hurry up,' shouted TT. 'We're pressed for time.'

Tallula climbed into the van and fitted herself into the cramped space with difficulty.

Filth stopped fiddling with the radio, looked over his shoulder and said, 'You all right back there, Tallula?'

'Fine,' said Tallula. 'Just fine.'

She wasn't, actually. There were no windows, it was dark and stuffy and the piano pedals dug painfully into her back, but she didn't want to cause a fuss.

The van jerked forward and her head banged sharply on the roof. She huddled down lower, wishing she had a cushion.

'What d'you think of the van, then?' howled TT over the noise of the engine.

'Great!' shouted Tallula. The van picked up speed, bumping over stones and finding every pothole. It came out as 'G-g-great!'

'Like the wording on the side?'

'I d-do,' said Tallula. Although she had noticed that her own name was conspicuous by its absence. She had a feeling that she would have to prove herself before *and a Werewolf Girl* was added.

'You missed having your photo taken,' bellowed TT.

'That's all r-right.'

Tallula was glad about that. She hated having her photo taken with normal-sized people. Either she stood up straight and her head got chopped off, or she crouched down to everyone else's height, which just looked silly.

'O'Brian wouldn't have his taken either,' said Arthur. 'He's camera-shy.'

O'Brian glared morosely out of the window and hugged his Pot. The seat he had chosen had a spring sticking up. He was trying to sit with his knees bent to one side to avoid it but he knew it was only a matter of time before it ripped his trousers.

A horrible crackling noise filled the air. Filth had got the radio working. He fiddled with the knobs and the crackling was replaced by a smooth voice.

'. . . *and a fine sunny day everywhere, especially at Sludgehaven-On-Sea, where temperatures have reached an all-time high. The time is ten o'clock. You have been listening to the weather forecast with Michael Prawn and it's now over to DJ Benny Bonkers for Bonkers' Half Hour!'*

At this point a new, shrill, overexcited voice took over.

'*Hey! Thanks very much, Michael, and hi there, boys*

and girls! H-e-e-e-re's Benny, all ready to play your favourite sounds! Let's hope the good weather lasts for tomorrow, when I'm off to sunny Sludgehaven for the Battle of the Bands. Talking of that, we'll start with one of the competing groups. Rodney and the Rattles are in the studio, boys and girls! Hey, Rodney, great to have you here. Feeling confident?'

There was a pause. Then a third voice spoke. It had a sneering, unpleasant quality.

'Well, obviously.'

'Good, good, great, terrific! Five bands are entering. Feel threatened by the competition?'

'No.'

'Ha, ha, that's confidence for you! Reckon your fans will turn out to support you?'

'Well, obviously.'

'Excellent! Good! Terrific! I'm guessing a lot of them will be tuned in right now. Any message for them?'

'No. Will this take much longer?'

'Er – no, I guess that's it. Well, good to talk to you, thanks for coming in. I know you and the band are pressed for time, but I believe you're going to do a quick number for us before you set off, right?'

At this point, the road dipped sharply and the radio started the hideous crackling again.

'Do something!' shouted TT. 'I want to hear what the competition's like!'

Filth fiddled with the knob and the crackling was replaced by silence.

'Lost the reception,' he said. 'Sorry.'

'I wonder if they've really got lots of fans,' said Arthur, sounding a bit anxious.

'So what if they have?' asked TT.

'Well – we haven't.'

'That's all you know.' TT snapped open the glove compartment, took out a large brown envelope and thrust it at Arthur. 'Here. Fan mail. Arrived this morning.'

'Oh my!' said Arthur. A couple of little sparks shot from his nose. 'How exciting!'

He reached into the envelope and drew out three smaller envelopes. They were decorated with hearts and sprinkled with silver glitter.

'Read them out, then,' said TT.

Arthur opened the first one.

'*dere filth i am yor bigest fan can i hav yor autogarf luv charlene.*'

'Well, that's nice, isn't it?' said TT. 'What's the next one say?'

Arthur opened the next one.

'*dere filth i am yor bigest fan can i hav yor autogarf luv jemella.*'

'R-i-i-i-ght,' said TT carefully. 'Also very nice. And the third?'

'*dere filth i am yor*—' Arthur broke off. 'Look, I don't know why I'm bothering. They're all for Filth.'

Crossly, he shoved the letters back into the envelope and thrust it at Filth, who gave an uninterested shrug and carried on fiddling with the radio.

'You'll have to reply,' said TT.

'No way,' said Filth.

'Well, somebody has to. You can't let your fans down.'

'Don't look at me,' said Arthur huffily. 'I'm not answering his silly fan mail for him.'

'Nor me,' said O'Brian. It was the first time he had spoken in ages. He shuffled around irritably in his seat. There came the distinct sound of trousers ripping.

'It's not the manager's job,' said TT firmly. 'I've got enough to do as it is. And I don't think Chip wants to do it, do you, Chip?'

'Uh,' grunted Chip, shaking his head.

'I'll do it if you like,' said Tallula from the back. 'Just show me how you sign your name and I'll forge it.'

Everyone looked startled. She had been so quiet, they had all forgotten she was there.

'There you go!' cried TT. 'Problem sorted. The Wer— Tallula'll do it.'

'Cool,' said Filth. 'Thanks, Tallula.'

Arthur threw the envelope over his shoulder. It landed in Tallula's lap. She smoothed it out and put it carefully to one side. She was glad to have a little job she could do for Filth, even if it was answering fan mail from other girls. Out of all the Boys, Filth was her favourite. She felt they had something important in common. Neither of them was in it for the fame or the money. It was all about the music. Besides, he was really cute.

'Ridiculous,' muttered Arthur, still put out. 'He should answer his own fan mail. Shouldn't he, O'Brian?'

'Right,' said O'Brian sulkily. To add to his woes, he was already feeling carsick. He tried winding down the window, but the handle came off in his hand.

'Man,' said Filth, sitting back from the radio with a sigh. 'I can't get it to work. Think it's dead.'

'That's all right,' said TT cheerfully. 'We'll just have to talk to each other.'

There was silence. Not a great start to what was going to be a long, long journey.

Tallula said brightly, 'Anyone fancy a biscuit?'

Chapter Fourteen

Preparations

We all know what it's like to spend hours and hours cooped up in a car. It's boring beyond belief. Let's just skip that bit and shoot on ahead a few hours. More interesting things are happening in Sludgehaven.

Ali Pali and the Mayor stood in warm late afternoon sunshine, surveying the field. Despite days of frantic activity, it was far from ready. The stage was still in the process of being erected. Teams of Gnomes in dungarees were scuttling around with ladders, lengths of cable and long planks of wood. On either side of the stage were two tents. One – the sparkly one with the fairy lights – was labelled CELEBRITIES. The second – big, white and ordinary – was for the BANDS.

Around the edge of the field, tents and stalls were springing up. A big tattooed Zombie and his big tattooed son were testing out the sound system. From everywhere came the relentless sound of hammering.

'ONE-TWO!' boomed the Zombie into a microphone. 'TURN IT UP, DAVE, IT NEEDS MORE TREBLE. ONE-TWO! ONE-TWO!'

'I hope this isn't going to go on much longer,' fretted the Mayor. 'We have strict noise regulations. As Mayor, it is my duty to enforce them.'

The Mayor was small. So small he stood on tiptoe to compensate. He had a mousy moustache and that horrible hairstyle that consists of a few strands grown really long and combed over a shiny bald pate. His chain of office was intended for someone much taller and clonked against his knees. That didn't stop him wearing it, though. It made him feel important. Feeling important was important to the Mayor.

'No, no,' Ali reassured him. 'All will be finished by sundown, Mr Mayor. You have my word. Now. Tell me. What do you think of your exclusive celebrity hospitality tent? It is my own design.'

'Well – very nice,' admitted the Mayor. 'Very – glittery. I can see that.'

'Everyone can,' said Ali happily. 'It is the sequins.'

'Yes,' said the Mayor. 'There are certainly plenty of those.'

'If there is one thing we Genies know about it is sequins.'

'That's as may be,' said the Mayor, 'but it's the noise I'm bothered about. I don't want complaints from the residents. As Mayor, I have to answer to them, you know.'

'There are no residents,' Ali pointed out mildly. 'This is a field.'

'Yes, but sound travels.' The Mayor's watery little eyes roamed around. 'I thought you said there would be spellovision cameras. I don't see any.'

'Arriving tomorrow.'

'Where will I sit? As Mayor, people will want to see me. Will I have a special chair?'

'Of course. There will be a special judging table. You, the Mystery Celebrities and my humble self will assemble at eleven o'clock in the celebrity tent, where a range of delicious food and drink will be available. There will be photo opportunities and the press will be wanting interviews. At twelve on the dot, the Battle begins. The popular radio DJ Benny Bonkers will open the proceedings. At his signal, we shall parade forth and take our places, to great rejoicing.'

'And who are these Mystery Celebrities? As Mayor, I think I should be told.'

'Ah. Now, there I have excellent news. This is for your ears only.'

Ali leaned over and whispered in the Mayor's ear, then stood back, looking smug.

'Really?' gasped the Mayor, his eyes widening. 'Well, well. My word. Quite a coup. As Mayor, I congratulate you.'

'Thank you.'

'Scott Sinister,' murmured the Mayor. 'Lulu Lamarre. Well, well.'

He pictured himself sitting between the famous stars, hopefully propped up higher with cushions. Chatting informally. Laughing uproariously. Having his picture taken with his arm resting lightly on Lulu Lamarre's luscious shoulders.

Like many people, the Mayor had a weakness for celebrities. He knew all about Scott Sinister, of course. He had read articles about him in back copies of *Famous and Fabulous* in the dentist's waiting room. He knew even more about Lulu Lamarre, Scott's equally famous, glamorous on-off girlfriend.

Interestingly, both stars had connections to Sludgehaven. Early on in their careers, they had both starred in a memorable summer show at the

Pier Pavilion. Since then, they had gone on to greater things, of course. But the Mayor was proud of the fact that Sludgehaven had played a small part in their rise to stardom. He intended to bring that up a *lot*.

'You seem surprised,' observed Ali.

'I am,' admitted the Mayor. 'I was under the impression that they had finally ended their – er – association. A lot of bad feeling between them, I was told. Not that I read the celebrity magazines myself, of course. I heard it from my secretary.'

'A little mild professional jealousy,' said Ali, with a shrug. 'It happens. Besides, neither of them knows that the other will be there. I thought it best not to mention it.'

'Is that wise? Won't they be upset?'

'Relax, Mr Mayor,' soothed Ali. 'They know the drill. When the cameras roll, they will put on happy, smiling faces, you will see. And they will be sitting alongside your good self. You are an important man. They are most anxious to meet you. Lulu in particular.'

'Really?' said the Mayor excitedly. 'She told you that?'

'Oh yes. All will be well, have no fear. I have booked them separate apartments at the Ritz. They arrive tonight. And then, tomorrow – let Battle commence!'

'Mmm,' said the Mayor. His eyes wandered again around the busy field. 'Well, let us hope it won't be too noisy. Those microphones are very loud. There have already been angry letters in the *Sludeghaven Times*. This is a respectable town, Mr Pali. A quiet little haven for families. Peaceful pleasures. A gentle paddle, a stroll along the promenade, a cream tea followed by an early night. We are attracting a better class of visitor these days. We don't encourage riff-raff.'

'Music lovers,' said Ali mildly. 'Loving families and loyal supporters. And they will be here, in the field. Well away from the town itself.'

'Let us hope so. The residents have made their feelings very clear.'

'They will feel differently when they see their Mayor on the spellovison, though,' said Ali. He gave the Mayor a little nudge. 'Sitting on an important judging panel. Flanked by famous superstars. Picture in the paper. Eh?'

'Well – yes,' agreed the Mayor more cheerfully. 'That's true.'

'Tomorrow will be your finest hour, Mr Mayor. You have my word.'

Over by the stage, one of the Gnomes in dungarees fell off a ladder with a resounding crash.

'ONE-TWO!' boomed the tattooed Zombie. 'MORE VOLUME, DAVE. ONE-TWO!'

The Mayor winced. There was no way the preparations would be completed by sundown. In the morning, his desk would be awash with more complaining letters.

But he wasn't going to be at his desk tomorrow, was he? He was going to be on spellovision. He was going to hobnob with superstars in a glittery tent. He was going to be a judge in an important music festival.

It was a shame he didn't like music. But at least it would get him out of the office and into the limelight. You had to take the rough with the smooth.

Chapter Fifteen
The Ritz

TT stood in the foyer of the Ritz hotel, staring around. He liked what he saw. Potted plants. Marble statues. Swishy velvet curtains. Deep sofas. Soft piped music. Oh yes. This would do. This would do very nicely.

'Yes? Can I help you?'

The voice came from behind the polished reception desk. It belonged to a Ghoul in a suit. He had a long, pale face and looked like he polished his hair with boot blacking.

'Your finest apartment for six,' said TT, producing his Magic Card and slamming it down with a flourish. 'I want a balcony, a trouser press and tea-making facilities. Oh, and a large spello to throw out of the window.' The Ghoul raised an eyebrow. 'Well, we might. Or we might not. We might just watch it. Either way, don't worry, I'll pay for any damage. As you see, I have this Magic Card.'

'You have booked, I take it?'

'What?' TT mentally ran through his list of things to do. Booking the Ritz had been the last item. He had *meant* to do it, of course, but what with the excitement of getting the band van and the Magic Card and packing . . .

'Well?' The Ghoul stared at him, waiting.

'Well – no,' confessed TT. 'It slipped my mind.'

'Can't be done, sir,' sighed the Ghoul. 'I don't know if you are aware, but there is some sort of . . . *musical* activity happening tomorrow.'

'The Battle of the Bands – yes, I know. That's why we're here. We're *The Witchway Rhythm Boys*. You may have heard of us?'

'No,' said the Ghoul. 'Not really my sort of thing. Anyway, we're fully booked.'

'Fetch the manager,' said TT.

'I *am* the manager.'

'Oh. Right.' TT scratched his head. 'Well, I'm a manager too. As one manager to another, can't we manage to sort this out?'

'I cannot conjure rooms out of fairy dust, sir.

If you'll excuse me, I have things to do. Important guests are arriving this evening.'

'So what am I supposed to *do*?' cried TT.

'Well, you could try finding a bed and breakfast. But I don't hold out too much hope at this late stage.'

'Ah, come on!' begged TT. 'You must have space somewhere. There's only six of us. Me, a Fiend, a Dragon, a Leprechaun, a Troll and a Werewolf. Oh, and my goldfish.'

'No pets,' said the Manager. 'Hotel policy.'

'He's a fish, not a mountain lion.'

'No pets.'

'All right! All right, he'll stay in the van. He'll be all right for one night. Look, work with me here. I promised everyone we'd stay at the Ritz.'

'Wish I could help, sir.'

'I'm begging. I'll get on my knees if you like.'

'Go on, then,' said the Ghoul. TT got down on his knees. The Ghoul inspected him. 'No. Doesn't help, sorry.'

It was stalemate. TT scrambled to his feet, snatched up the Magic Card and was just about to storm out when he thought of something else.

'Suppose I pay double?'

'No.'

'Triple?'

'Try again.'

'All right, *four times*. Four times the usual amount.'

The Ghoul rolled his eyes and waited.

'Five?'

The Ghoul waited.

'OK then, six. Final offer.'

'Ah!' said the Ghoul. 'I've just remembered. There *is* somewhere. You might just be able to squeeze in. But it doesn't have a trouser press.'

'TT's taking his time,' said Arthur.

The five of them sat in the van, staring out at the dark hotel car park. Well, all except Tallula, who had no window to look out of.

It had been a long journey and everyone was tired, achy and hungry. Filth's cheese sandwiches hadn't gone very far between six and nobody wanted any of Arthur's mustard ones. Tallula's biscuits hadn't lasted long. The radio still refused to work. They had tried playing I Spy, but TT drove so fast that by the time they had spied something it had shot by, so they were limited to the van's interior. D for Dragon. G for Goldfish. P for Pot. T for Troll. It had got really boring.

They had stopped three times, twice for O'Brian to be carsick and once to fill up with petrol at a small service station high up in the Misty Mountains. It was run by a bad-tempered Hobgoblin who charged the earth for egg rolls and mistook O'Brian for a Pixie. Otherwise, it was just long hours of relentless driving.

Their spirits had lifted when they finally reached the top of the mountains and caught a faraway glimpse of the sea – but it had taken another hour to reach Sludgehaven. The sun had already dipped below the horizon as they drove slowly through the town, looking for the Ritz. A full moon was rising over the rooftops. The streets were deserted. It seemed that the town's residents believed in going to bed early.

'Are you *sure* all the biscuits have gone, Tallula?' asked Arthur.

'Yes,' said Tallula. 'Sorry.'

Her biscuits had proved very popular, except with O'Brian, who had predictably choked on his and had to be thumped on the back.

'Here he comes,' said Arthur as TT came marching back triumphantly towards the van.

'All right, everyone out,' shouted TT. 'It's all sorted. I've got us a room. Not quite what I had in mind. No trouser press, I'm afraid. But it's nice and cosy.'

A short while later, the six of them stood clustered in the doorway, examining the room.

'This is it?' enquired Arthur.

'Yes,' said TT. 'This is it.'

'It isn't a bedroom. It's the boiler room.'

'Yes,' said TT. 'I know. It's all they had.'

Everyone stared silently at the jungle of pipes that filled the room. A single light bulb dangled from a frayed flex, casting a dim light over the antique boiler that roared away in the middle. As well as containing the boiler, the room doubled as a dumping ground for the hotel junk – mouldering rolls of carpet, a pile of ancient mattresses propped against the wall, a heap of rusty old paint tins, boxes of chipped crockery.

'It's dirty,' said Arthur. He ran a fastidious claw along a ledge. 'See? Dirt. Cobwebs. Spiders.'

'So what's a spider or two between friends?' cried TT. 'Look on the bright side. At least we don't have to waste energy wrecking it. Right, let's get sorted. Chip, move those tins, find us a bit of floor space. We'll get these mattresses spread out. Make ourselves comfortable, eh?'

Nobody made a move except Chip, who spat on his hands and set about kicking tins into corners.

'I'll take this one,' announced TT, pouncing on the biggest mattress and dragging it as far away as he could from the raging boiler. 'Come on, come on. It's a bit like camping, right? Anybody ever camped? No? Well, I'm telling you, it's a whole lot of fun.'

'I very much doubt that,' said Arthur.

'Ah, come on. You'll love it.'

'No, I *won't*,' insisted Arthur. 'I want clean sheets and a proper bed.'

'Look,' said TT. 'Give me a break, eh? I've been driving all day. All right, I admit I should have booked in advance, but I can't think of everything.'

'That's what a manager is supposed to do,' said Arthur. 'It wouldn't have happened if *I* was running things.'

'*Nothing* happened when you were running things,' pointed out TT. 'We're here, aren't we? And tomorrow we're going to win the Battle of the Bands. What's the big fuss? It's only for one night.'

'He's right,' said Filth. 'Chill, Arthur, it's a room, dude. It'll do.' He stepped into the room and began examining the pile of mattresses. 'Hey, O'Brian, come and choose yours, man.'

O'Brian eyed the pile of mattresses without enthusiasm. He knew he'd end up with the worst one, so why bother?

Only Tallula remained hovering in the doorway. TT looked up, saw her and gave an exasperated sigh. Of course. She was a girl. Sure to make a fuss.

'Something wrong?' he enquired. 'Not good enough for you?'

'Not big enough, actually,' said Tallula.

Everyone stopped what they were doing and looked round. She was right. There was no way she was going to fit in. None of the mattresses was long enough, for a start. And the room had a very low ceiling.

'She's got a point, man,' said Filth. 'Where's Tallula gonna sleep, dude?'

'It's OK,' said Tallula. 'I'll sleep in the van. I don't mind.'

'There you go!' cried TT. 'She'll sleep in the van. Problem sorted.'

'You sure, Tallula?' said Filth.

'Yes. I'll be fine.'

'Of course you will,' said TT. 'Oh – and see if you can rustle up a few sandwiches on your way out. Get a selection.'

'Cheese for me,' said Filth.

'Chilli and mustard,' said Arthur. 'O'Brian?'

'Don't care,' muttered O'Brian.

'All right,' said Tallula. 'I'll see what I can do.'

'*Sleep in the van*,' said TT, as her footsteps padded away. 'Ha!'

'What's that supposed to mean?' said Arthur.

'Ah, come *on*. She's a Werewolf, isn't she? There's a full moon out there. I'll bet you anything you like she'll be running over the clifftops baying at it, because that's what Werewolves do.'

'She said she, like, makes biscuits,' said Filth.

'Yes, I know. She *said* that. But the shops are closed now. Where will she get the ingredients?'

'I don't care what she does,' said Arthur, 'as long as she doesn't wear her voice out for tomorrow.'

Tallula padded through reception. Nobody was behind the desk. She was just about to ring the bell when she saw the sign. It said:

**ROOM SERVICE CANCELLED.
FAMOUS CELEBRITIES EXPECTED.**

Some hotel, thought Tallula. She wondered whether to go back and tell the Boys – but what was the point? They would find out soon enough. Besides, she needed to get out.

She stepped through the big doors and paused on the top step to take in the night. It was cool. It was dark. The huge moon hung in the sky. There was nobody around. It was the perfect night for a long, leisurely run. In the distance, she could hear the swish of the sea. Somewhere, there would be high cliffs.

Should she? She was certainly tempted.

But, no. It was a big day tomorrow. Better to stick with a short jog, maybe along the promenade. Shake out all the aches, breathe some good sea air, then crawl into the van and hopefully get some sleep.

She padded down the steps and set off at an easy lope.

No sooner had she gone than a long, low limousine came purring up the street.

Chapter Sixteen
Consulting
the Oracle

'I hope Gareth's all right,' said TT. 'He seemed a bit quiet when we left him.'

There was a little pause while everyone thought about this. They were all spread out on their mattresses. Arthur had fastidiously covered his with a million tissues and was trying to keep his tail from touching the floor. Filth lay on his back, eyes closed, tapping out a little rhythm on his tummy. O'Brian was curled around his Pot. Only Chip was asleep and giving out deep, gravelly snores. Occasionally he gave a little jerk and muttered 'Uh? Uh!' Obviously having some sort of Trollish dream conversation.

'He's always quiet,' said Arthur, after a bit. 'He's a fish.'

'That doesn't mean he's not communicating.'

'So *you* say.'

'Well, it's true. Watch the bubbles.'

Arthur was feeling argumentative and wasn't prepared to let this go.

'Why? What's in the bubbles?'

'Everything. Say anything you like and he'll give you feedback.'

'Feedback!' snorted Arthur. '*Feedback!* What about you, O'Brian? Have *you* noticed anything in Gareth's bubbles apart from regurgitated ant eggs? The Meaning Of Life, perhaps?'

O'Brian said nothing. He was at an all-time low. Curled up in a sullen ball of misery on the worst mattress, which of course was full of lumps and bumps and had springs sticking out *everywhere*. Hugging his Pot. Imprisoned in a pink T-shirt, trousers torn, hot, queasy and plagued with a guilty secret. Right now, he didn't want to get drawn into the conversation. If he spoke, he might break down and blab it all out.

'Well, I'm sorry, but I don't believe you,' went on Arthur. 'He's just a fish.'

'You're wrong,' insisted TT earnestly. 'I should know – I live with him. He's not at all judgemental. It's a big comfort to get things off your chest to Gareth. He's got his head screwed on the right way.'

'Just as well,' smirked Arthur. 'If it was on the wrong way, he'd be facing his tail.'

'You can laugh,' said TT. 'Oh yes, you can laugh.'

'Man, it's *hot* in here,' sighed Filth.

It was too. Even for Fiends and Dragons, who like the warmth. Hot, crowded and uncomfortable. The boiler was blasting out heat like there was no tomorrow. Above their heads, the pipes rattled and banged in a cacophony of dodgy plumbing.

'No sign of the sandwiches,' said Arthur irritably. 'D'you think Tallula forgot to ask?'

'I'll bet she did,' said TT. 'Got her mind on other things. Mark my words, she's up howling on the cliff right now. Once a Werewolf always a Werewolf. I don't care what she says, I know how the moon takes 'em.'

'Well, it's not my job to get the sandwiches,' said Arthur. 'You're the one with the manager's hat on.'

'I've been driving all day,' said TT. 'I got us a van and a roadie and a Magic Card, didn't I? I'm going to make you famous, right? I've managed to get us here and managed to get us a room. I've managed enough.'

'Take the hat off, then.'

'No,' said TT firmly. 'The hat stays on. O'Brian? What about you?'

O'Brian hugged his Pot to his chest and said nothing.

'I'll go,' said Filth. 'Could do with a breath of fresh air anyway.'

'You do that,' agreed TT. 'I don't know about anyone else, but I'm starving. Big day tomorrow. Need to keep our strength up. Oh – and just look in on Gareth, would you? I don't want him to feel he's been abandoned.'

Filth strolled into the foyer, which was a scene of great activity. Bellboys, maids and porters were scuttling around in a state of hysterical excitement. The source of the fuss was a tall figure dressed in a black silk robe lined with scarlet. He was surrounded by shiny suitcases and talking to the Ghoul at the reception desk. Although it was night-time, he was wearing sunglasses.

Filth knew who this was, of course. Scott Sinister, star of stage and screen. Everyone recognised *him*.

Most people would be impressed to be in the presence of one so famous, but Filth was one of those rare types who wasn't. He had a nifty little riff going around in his head that was far more interesting.

Everyone seemed a bit busy, so Filth decided to wait before enquiring about sandwiches. He would steer clear of the desk, pop out and cool down a bit, check on Gareth, then collar the manager on the way back in, when he wasn't so busy.

He stepped through the glass doors into the fresh night air. The full moon was wonderful. If TT was right and Tallula was off somewhere howling at it, he hoped it was doing her a power of good.

The band van was in the car park, next to a long, sleek limousine.

Filth sauntered over, pulled open the van door and climbed in.

The bowl sat on the dashboard in a pale shaft of moonlight. Gareth was suspended in the middle, fins gently moving, tail swishing slowly from side to side, looking inscrutable.

Filth leaned in close. He said, 'Hey. You OK, fish dude?'

There was a long pause where nothing happened. Then –

From out of Gareth's gaping mouth appeared a bubble. A big, cheery-looking bubble. It shot to the surface and popped in a minuscule explosion of air.

PLOP! Just like that.

'Yeah,' said Filth happily. 'Me too.'

Well, he was. Tomorrow he would be playing Crash 'n' Bang to a big audience in a big field, in the sunshine. For Filth, it was all about the music.

'So what about the sandwiches?' asked Arthur querulously as Filth came strolling back into the boiler room, which was hotter than ever. 'Are they sending them?'

'No,' said Filth. 'There's, like, a notice? Room service cancelled.'

'Cancelled?' Arthur exploded upright, sending his carefully placed tissues flying.

'That's what it said.' Filth threw himself back on to his mattress.

'You didn't complain to the manager?'

'Dude was busy. Scott Sinister's just arrived.'

'What?' gasped TT, sitting bolt upright. 'Scott Sinister? *Really?* Staying *here?* Why didn't you *say?*'

'I just did.'

'Oh my!' TT was beside himself with excitement. 'Wow! Hear that, boys? I love Scott Sinister! Those *Killer Poodle* films are *ace!* Arthur? O'Brian? Hear that? I've booked us into the same hotel as Scott Sinister!'

'Oh, that's all right then,' said Arthur. 'I wonder which room he's got? The broom cupboard, perhaps?'

'D'you know what I'm thinking?' went on TT. 'I'm thinking he's one of the Mystery Celebrities on the judging panel. It'd make sense if I went out there and introduced myself, don't you think? Shake his hand, tell him we're all big admirers, ask him to vote for us . . .'

'No,' said Filth firmly. 'Wouldn't be cool, dude.'

'Oh. Well, perhaps you're right. Did you check on Gareth?'

'Yeah. Says he's OK.'

'Good,' said TT. 'I thought he would be.'

There was a pause.

'What d'you mean, he *says* he's OK?' said Arthur.

'He's OK, OK?' Filth gave a yawn. 'Kinda excited about tomorrow, a bit on edge, but looking forward to it, you know? Sends everyone his regards.'

'I see,' sneered Arthur. 'That's what he *said*, is it?'

'You see?' said TT. 'I told you. Where are you going?' Arthur had climbed off his mattress and was heading out of the door.

'Where do you think? I'm going to complain to the management. The service here is terrible.'

The van shook as someone climbed into the driver's seat. The water in the fish bowl sloshed about a bit as whoever it was made themselves comfortable.

Gareth stopped swimming in mindless circles and faced the glass to receive his latest caller.

After a moment, a scaly purple face loomed towards him and a pair of hugely magnified eyes filled the horizon, like twin moons.

Gareth waited, fluttering his fins.

'Ahem.' The caller cleared his throat. 'Um – Gareth? It's – er – me. Arthur.'

Gareth waited.

'All well in fish world, is it?'

Gareth blew an affirmative bubble.

Plop.

'Would that be –' Arthur hesitated – 'a yes?'

Gareth blew another. There was a little pause.

'Good,' said Arthur. 'Good to know you're all right.' He gave a heavy sigh. 'I only wish I was.'

There was another little pause. Gareth waited.

'I'm probably being petty,' went on Arthur after a bit. 'It's just that – look, I know you're TT's pet and you have to be loyal, but – well, to be absolutely frank, I'm getting heartily sick of him taking *over*. I wasn't that bad a manager, after all. I got us gigs, didn't I? I kept the books balanced. I didn't go round with a stupid hat on, flashing Magic Cards and buying cameras and watches and booking us into five-star boiler rooms.'

Gareth blew a stream of small, questioning bubbles. *Plop-plop-pop?*

'Well, yes,' said Arthur. 'Yes, of *course* I want to win. And obviously I want a record contract – who wouldn't? But everything's happening so *fast*. It's all out of my control. Right now I just wish I was home eating one of Mam's curries, getting ready to do a local gig where nobody expects anything.'

PLOP! Gareth blew a big bubble of stout support.

'Well, I know that,' said Arthur. 'I know we're *good*. But are we good *enough*? We haven't heard the competition and some people – well, most people – just don't *get* Crash 'n' Bang. And we're not at our best right now. O'Brian's sulking and won't be parted from his Pot in case someone steals it. And Tallula's never been on a stage before so I'm worried about that. And I wouldn't admit this to anyone else, but I'm a bit hurt because I didn't get any fan mail although the piano's the most important instrument and after all I did *start* the band . . .'

And so it went on, for quite some time. Another large, sleek limousine drew up and parked alongside the first – but Arthur didn't even notice.

Some time later, Arthur came back into the boiler room. Everyone appeared to be asleep and snoring apart from the boiler, which was wide awake and roaring. He pulled the string hanging next to the bare light bulb and crept over to his mattress in the dark.

'You've been a while,' came O'Brian's voice.

'Yes,' said Arthur.

'Did you speak to the manager?'

'No. He's a bit tied up. Another celebrity's just arrived. Lulu Lamarre. She's out there signing auto-graphs for the staff. She has twenty-seven pieces of luggage. I counted.'

'So what took you so long, then?' asked O'Brian.

'I – er – checked on Gareth,' said Arthur. 'He – er – he says he's fine.'

Tallula lay curled up in the dark in the back of the van, wishing that the voice droning on in the front seat would talk a little more quietly. This was the *third* visitor to the van and it seemed that he was going to be there for some time. Despite stuffing her fingers in her ears, she could hear every word.

'. . . And everything keeps going wrong, simply everything. Ever since I wouldn't mend the Fairy's shoes. It was bad enough turning a job down – Leprechauns aren't supposed to do that. But it was the *way* I did it, Gareth. I was rude. I shouted. Mocked her taste in music. That's why she's got it in for me. I can see her now, laughing in her little mushroom house, waving her vicious little wand, sending me misfortune after misfortune. And it's not going to stop. You know what'll happen tomorrow, don't you? I won't be able to stop my feet skipping and I'll look even sillier than usual. And my fingers are bandaged so I'll mess up the solo and we'll lose the Battle of the Bands and *it'll be all my fault*! And another thing. I'm worried about the Pot. It's going to get stolen, I just know it. I've managed to hang on to it so far, but it's only a matter of time. She's saving that for last. I'll go home without it and be the laughing stock of the Leprechaun world . . .'

And so it went on . . .

And on . . .

And on.

Chapter Seventeen

A New Day Dawns

Scott Sinister sat in the dining room of the Ritz hotel, waiting for his breakfast to arrive. He had ordered the works – cereal, grapefruit, a full fry-up, toast, marmalade, a selection of jams and coffee. Well, why not? He wasn't paying.

The dining room was deserted. Scott didn't like to be pestered by autograph hunters at mealtimes. At his insistence, the management had placed a notice on the dining-room door. It said:

CELEBRITIES ONLY.
CLOSED TO THE PUBLIC.

He shook out the local paper that had been

thoughtfully placed on the table and examined the headline on the front page. It screamed:

EXCLUSIVE! MYSTERY CELEBRITIES REVEALED!

Scott gave a pleased little smile and read on.

We can finally reveal the identity of the Mystery Celebrities who will be helping judge today's Battle of the Bands competition. Last night, our reporter observed the arrival of two limousines at the exclusive Ritz hotel. First to arrive was Scott Sinister, star of stage and screen!

That's me, thought Scott happily. He loved seeing his name in the paper.

The second limousine, which arrived shortly after, contained the second Mystery Celebrity, who turns out to be —

Just at that moment, the dining-room door burst open. Scott looked up eagerly, expecting his breakfast.

It wasn't, though.

'*You!*' snarled Scott, throwing down the paper and starting to his feet.

'*You!*' hissed Lulu.

Not a great start to the day.

'I still can't believe they wouldn't serve us breakfast,' said Arthur. 'I'm sure it's against the law.'

'We'll get something when we get to the field,' promised TT. 'Right now, I need to concentrate on driving. Watch out for the signs. The big yellow arrows.'

'I hope they didn't charge the full amount,' went on Arthur. 'Did you pay with the Magic Card?'

'I did,' said TT. 'Don't you worry about it. I'm the manager – I deal with the finances.'

'I can't *help* worrying,' said Arthur. 'I don't trust that card of yours. I've never heard of a card that means you get everything for free. Suppose the Magic runs out?'

'Trust me, it won't,' said TT confidently. 'Anyway, we're all going to be millionaires soon.' He reached down beside the seat and came up with another large brown envelope. 'Stop worrying and read your fan mail.'

'There's more fan mail?'

'Yep. Picked it up from reception when I was paying.'

'Is it all for Filth?'

'Haven't looked. Probably.'

Arthur snatched the envelope and threw it over his shoulder.

'Here, Tallula,' he snapped. 'For you.'

Tallula caught the envelope and peered inside.

'There's three more for you, Filth,' she said. 'From those Banshee girls, by the look of it.'

'Oh, *man*,' sighed Filth.

'And there's a postcard for Arthur,' said Tallula.

'Really?' said Arthur, brightening up.

'It's from your mother. It's got a picture of a volcano.'

'Oh. Well, read it out, then.'

'*Dear son*,' read Tallula. '*I am missing you. Had a take-away lavaburger last night. No point cooking for one. Your loving Mam.*'

'Well, that's nice, isn't it?' said TT.

'Mmm,' said Arthur. He had mixed feelings about the postcard. It was nice to get it, of course, but it wasn't exactly fan mail. Besides, he didn't like to think of his mother sitting down to a lonely take-away. Suddenly, he felt a long way from home.

O'Brian leaned against the window with his eyes closed. Talking his troubles over with Gareth the night before hadn't helped as much as he had hoped. It had been good to get it off his chest, of course. But there had been no answers. No revelations. No hope for the future. He was on his own.

'There's a letter for you, O'Brian,' said Tallula unexpectedly.

What was this? O'Brian sat up. He had fan mail? For the first time in ages, he felt his depression lift a little.

'Shall I read it out?'

'Yes, yes, read it out,' said O'Brian.

'*Dear O'Brian,*' read Tallula. '*You weren't answering your phone so me and the boys called round to check. Your Rainbow Deflector's been stolen. The garden's been stripped bare of shamrock and clover. Goblins have broken in and are squatting in the workshop. They've eaten all your food and have been kicking the shoes around and putting them back in all the wrong boxes . . .*' Tallula broke off. 'Um – do you want me to go on?'

'Finish it,' said O'Brian dully.

'It's just that there's quite a bit more . . .'

'I said finish it!' shouted O'Brian. Tallula bent her head back to the letter.

'*. . . so we chased them away but we think they'll come back because they're hiding in the bushes and laughing. Also we bumped into Witch Sludgegooey, who says you've gone running off with your daft band to play that awful music you like so much in some faraway field. She says you have taken to wearing a pink T-shirt, of all things. You are a disgrace to the Leprechauns. Kind regards, your brother Paddy.*

P.S. We noticed the Pot's missing. Sludgegooey says you've taken it with you. Are you mad? Is a music festival any kind of place to take a pot of valuable gold? If it gets stolen, you're for it. Return home immediately and explain yourself.

There was a long pause. Then TT said, 'Hey! At least the sun's shining.'

Chapter Eighteen

In the Tents

The Battle of the Bands was due to start at noon, but already there was a long queue stretching back from the main gates along the fences that enclosed the field. Hardened music fans know that you have to arrive early if you want to be near the action.

The band van crawled past the gates, where the turnstile was busily clicking and five-pound notes were briskly changing hands. There was huge placard attached to the gates. It read:

BATTLE OF THE BANDS!
ENTRY £5
STRICTLY NO FIGHTING!

TT was so excited that he almost didn't see the tattooed Zombie who stepped into the road, frantically waving an arm. It had separated at the shoulder so he held it with his other hand and was using it to point with.

Behind the stage, a cordoned-off parking area had been set aside. Three vans had already arrived. One was pink, and had *The Gnomettes* emblazoned across the side in flowery writing. One was an evil green and announced *Betty and the Bully Girls* in big, threatening letters. The third was grey and had nothing written on it. It probably belonged to *One Big Troll and Some Other Biggish Ones* as, sadly, Trolls can't spell and are therefore doomed for eternity to ride around in unmarked vans.

'Here we all are, then,' said TT, edging the van through the gate and accidentally running over the Zombie's foot. 'Looks like most of the competition's beaten us to it.' He pulled on the brake and switched off the engine. 'Right, everybody out.'

In the back, Tallula began the complicated process of unfolding herself from her dark little cave. This was it, then. No going back now. The doors opened and light streamed in, making her blink. She stretched out her endless hairy legs and climbed out into the sunshine, where Arthur and O'Brian were having an argument. Arthur wanted O'Brian to leave the Pot in the van and O'Brian was insisting on taking it with him.

'It'll just draw attention,' snapped Arthur.

'I'm keeping it with me.'

'It'll be safer in the van.'

'I'm keeping it with me.'

'Ah, let him,' said Filth. 'Whatever. If it makes him happy, dude. Me, I'm for a sandwich.'

The band tent was packed, but the atmosphere was strained. There was clearly no intermingling going on. The rival bands stood around muttering in little cliques, casting unfriendly looks over their shoulders at the opposition.

Ignoring the nudges and unfriendly stares, the Boys, Chip and TT made a beeline for the food table. Or, rather, the no-food table. All the plates were empty of everything but a single forlorn, squashed fairy cake sitting in a sea of crumbs. Musicians always have enormous appetites, but apparently nobody had informed the caterers.

'Man,' sighed Filth. 'No food, dudes. Wouldn't you just know it?' He wandered over to the large tea urn at the end of the table and pressed the button without much hope. As expected, it had run out.

'No chairs either,' said Arthur glumly. 'I can't say I'm impressed. No food, nowhere to sit, not even a napkin. Where's the hospitality in that?'

O'Brian said nothing. He didn't like the looks he was getting. It was either the stupid T-shirt or, more likely, the Pot. Fiercely, he clutched it even more tightly to his chest.

Three female Gnomes in pink frilly dresses with matching shoes and handbags were standing in a sniffy little group. All three wore dangling earrings in the shape of little fishes and had pink, beribboned fishing rods sticking out of their handbags. (Gnomes are into fishing in a big way – even the girls.) They were whispering and casting haughty looks over their shoulders at four tough-looking female Zombies with frightening hairstyles and heavy boots who were glaring back in a confrontational sort of way.

A collection of Trolls – one big, the others biggish – were busily scoffing handfuls of gravel from a big bowl. Gravel was clearly unpopular with the other bands. It was the only thing left on the table, apart from the fairy cake that nobody fancied.

Chip waddled over to join them. They all muttered 'Uh!' in greeting and gravely handed him the bowl, as is the Trollish way.

'*He's* all right, then,' said Arthur irritably.

All this time, Tallula had been hovering by the entrance, trying to pluck up courage to go in. She wasn't used to crowds. But she couldn't hang about for ever. Besides, an enormous bone-white bus with darkened windows was nosing into the car park. The writing on the side said *Rodney and the Rattles* and was accompanied by the picture of a sneering skull wearing sunglasses. She didn't want to be caught out in the open on her own.

She took a deep breath, smoothed down her horrible frock that was even more creased than usual, ducked under the doorway and went in.

The Gnomettes spotted her instantly. They nudged each other and smirked behind their hands.

'Oh my! Look at *her*!'

'Talk about *hairy*!'

'Just look at that dreadful *frock*!'

Stricken with embarrassment, Tallula looked around for somewhere to hide. There was a large potted plant standing in a corner and she made for that.

A murmur went up as a tall Skeleton wearing a dazzling white suit with massive shoulder pads came swaggering into the tent. He wore huge sunglasses and carried a banjo in his bony hand. He was closely followed by four slightly shorter Skeletons, also decked out in sunglasses and smart white suits and carrying banjos.

'Rodney,' hissed Arthur to TT.

General waves of dislike wafted in Rodney's direction as he stood sneering in a superior sort of way. *The Rattles* hovered at his hugely padded shoulders, attempting to sneer as effectively as their leader but not quite making it. Rodney was the undisputed master of superior sneering.

'Who's in charge here?' demanded Rodney. 'Where's Benny Bonkers?'

Shrugs all round. Even if they knew, they weren't about to tell him.

In the celebrities' tent, things weren't going too well either. The problem wasn't with the catering. In fact, the caterers had gone overboard. The table was heaped with all kinds of sumptuous food – strawberries, ice cream, chocolate cake, grapes, sandwiches, sugary biscuits, Turkish delight. The tea urn was up and running. There was a variety of cold drinks, including sherbet champagne.

The problem wasn't with the seating. There was a comfortable sofa with plumped-up cushions. There were footstools. There was a plush red carpet underfoot.

No. The problem was with the lack of Mystery Celebrities.

'Where are they?' demanded the Mayor, who had

arrived punctually despite being up all night polishing his chain. 'I thought you said they would be here.'

'Patience, Mr Mayor,' soothed Ali. 'Great artists cannot be hurried. Besides, it is fashionable to be late.'

'But I thought you said they were anxious to meet me? As Mayor, I don't like to be kept waiting.'

'They will come. Trust me. Have a banana.'

'I don't *want* a banana. As Mayor, I –'

'PALI!' The sudden, furious cry rang out. 'I'VE GOT A BONE TO PICK WITH YOU!'

'Ah,' said Ali. 'Scott. You have arrived. Allow me to introduce the Mayor of Slu—'

'Never mind about that!' roared Scott, advancing into the tent, ignoring the Mayor's hopefully extended hand. 'Why didn't you tell me? Of all the people in the world, you expect me to sit on the same panel as that – that mincing *amateur*?'

'Now then,' began Ali mildly. 'Calm yourself. Just simmer down and –'

'*Amateur?*' came an outraged shriek. 'Did you just call me an *amateur*, Scott Sinister?'

'Ah,' beamed Ali. 'Lulu, darling. How lovely you look this morning. Allow me to introduce the M—'

'How *could* you?' screeched Lulu. She brushed past the Mayor, skewering his foot with a spiked shoe. 'How *could* you, Ali! I would *never* have agreed! *Never!* Not if I'd known *he* was on the panel. Stuck-up swankpot.'

The Mayor was hopping around in agony but nobody cared. He threw himself on to the sofa and moaned quietly, rubbing his foot.

'You see?' roared Scott. 'You *see* what I have to put up with? Do you know what this crazed creature did? She attacked me at breakfast! With crumpets!'

'Crumpets,' mused Ali. 'A tasty snack, but personally, for breakfast I prefer croissants. Although those little miniature muffins are –'

'There was *jam* on them! There was *jam* in my *hair*! The woman is *mad*, I tell you! There is no way, absolutely no way I'm sitting on the same panel as a madwoman.'

'*Poodle boy!*' snarled Lulu. 'I've seen your film! All you do is get mauled by little puppies!'

'And I've seen your show! *Singalongalulu!* Ha! *Yawnalongarubbish*, more like.'

'You hear that? You hear what he just said? Tell him, Ali!'

'Tell *her!*' bawled Scott. 'And will somebody stop that little man *moaning*. It's getting on my nerves!'

'Er – excuse me?' said a voice. A bespectacled face was peering into the tent. It belonged to a solemn-looking Imp with a notebook in his hand. 'Denzil Pencil, reporter with *Famous and Fabulous*. Just wondering if now's a good time for an interview? I've got the photographer here.'

'Perfect timing,' purred Ali. 'Come in, Mr Pencil, come in. Scott? Lulu? Ready for the press?'

'By all means,' said Scott graciously. 'That is, if *you* are, Lulu, sweetheart?'

'Why, of course,' said Lulu. She gave a merry little laugh and tossed her hair. 'Come along, Mr Mayor. Come and stand with me and Scotty. We're all going to have our picture taken! Won't that be fun? Ali, darling, come and stand here – you should be in it too.'

Celebrities, eh?

Back in the bands' tent, Filth pushed his way through the rabble of musicians. In his hand was a paper plate containing the squashed fairy cake. He squeezed behind the potted palm and held it out to Tallula.

'Want it? It's the only thing left. Nobody, like, fancies it.'

'Neither do I, actually,' said Tallula. 'But – thanks.'

'I guess we could always chuck it at Rodney,' said Filth in an attempt to make her smile. She didn't, though. She just brushed the hair out of her eyes and gave a heavy sigh.

'So what's, like, with the, like, hiding thing?' enquired Filth after a bit.

'They're staring at me,' said Tallula.

'Who is?'

'Everyone. Well, mainly *The Gnomettes*. They're laughing at my frock. I can't say I blame them. Even *I* hate it. I know I should get a new one. But I don't like shopping. It's the mirrors in the changing rooms. They make me look awful.'

'Aw, come on,' said Filth. 'You look OK.'

'No, I don't. You don't have to pretend. I'm tall and hairy and nothing ever fits. *I* don't fit. I shouldn't have come. I'm a *Werewolf*. I don't know what I'm even doing here.'

'You're here to sing,' said Filth. 'It's all about the music, right?'

'Well, yes, but –'

'Forget the frock. Just do what you do. Walk out on that stage and *wow* 'em.'

'You really think so?'

'For real.' Filth held out his hand. 'Come on. It'll be fun.'

Shyly, Tallula reached down and took his hand and together they stepped out into the tent. Nobody noticed them. All eyes were currently on the latest arrival, who came bustling in armed with a clipboard, shouting '*Heeeeeere's Benny!*' just in case anyone was in doubt.

DJ Benny Bonkers was short, pink and wildly enthusiastic. He wore a romper suit with stars on and his spiky hair was dyed orange. When you looked at him, the word 'overexcitable' came to mind.

'Right, boys and girls!' bellowed DJ Benny Bonkers. 'Let's get this show on the road! Gather round and listen up. We kick off in ten minutes. I take the stage, whip the crowd into a frenzy, bring on the judges, all that. Then we're off. Each band does one number only, no encores. You wait for the judges' comments, then clear the stage ready for the next band. Any questions?'

'What's the running order?' shouted one of the *Bully Girls*.

'First up are the *Trolls*, followed by *The Gnomettes*, then *Betty and the Bully Girls*, then *Rodney and the Rattles*, and we finish up with *The Witchway Rhythm Boys*.'

There was some grumbling at this. *Rodney and the Rattles* were particularly vigorous with their complaints. Only the *Trolls* looked happy. Everyone wanted to go first, while the crowds were still fresh and enthusiastic. DJ Benny Bonkers explained that he had put all the band names into a hat and drawn them out at random, because that was the fairest way.

'So we're on last,' said Arthur to TT. 'Is that good, do you think?'

'It's *very* good,' said TT. 'The rubbish goes on first, leading up to the grand climax. That's you.'

'Yes, but what if people get bored and leave? We don't have any fans of our own. I've just had a peek out front and there isn't a single banner for us.'

'But they haven't *heard* you yet, have they? They've got that pleasure to come. And everyone will stay to the end to hear the result. Are you telling me you're losing faith in Crash 'n' Bang?'

'Well, no, but —'

'There you are then. You've got to think like a winner. Impressing the judges, that's what matters. Stop fretting, Arthur. You're letting the nerves get to you. Hey! It looks like someone's come to fix the tea urn. I'm getting in the queue.' And he bustled off.

Filth and Tallula wandered up to join Arthur.

'Hey, man,' said Filth. 'Where's O'Brian?'

'Gone back to the van.' Arthur gave a sigh. 'I'm worried about him. He's been acting very peculiar. I don't think the letter from home helped.'

'Yeah, right. Dude does seem to having a lot of bad luck. For a Leprechaun.'

'Weird,' said Arthur, shaking his head.

'Listen,' said Tallula. 'I'm not sure if I should tell you this, but there's something I think you should know . . .'

Chapter Nineteen

The Battle Begins

It was noon and the field was packed. The sun shone high in a cloudless blue sky, where seagulls swooped and wheeled and occasionally dropped little presents on people's shoulders. In front of the stage was a roped-off area containing the judging table set on the plinth. The families, friends and supporters of the competing bands were cheerfully brandishing their banners of support. Somebody had started up a slow handclap, but it sounded quite cheerful. There were a lot of silly hats on show, because where else can you wear a silly hat but at a music festival?

There came a buzz of anticipation followed by a huge cheer as DJ Benny Bonkers whizzed onstage and grabbed the microphone.

'Hello, Sludgehaven!' shouted Benny.

'Hello, Benny!' roared the crowd.

'That's me! DJ Benny Bonkers, your host for the day. Ready for some action?'

'Yeeeeeessssss!'

'Have we got a great line-up for you! Five new bands, no less, all ready to battle it out to be the first to sign on with the hot new record label *Genie Sounds*. But first, let's begin with a big Sludgehaven welcome for – *the judges*!'

The Vampire cameraman trained his camera on the glittering tent, the flap moved to one side – and there they were! The four famous celebrities. Well, let's be honest here – the three famous celebrities plus the Mayor. Ali Pali led the way with Scott and Lulu walking behind, blowing kisses and waving to the cheering crowds. The Mayor hobbled at the rear, trying not to trip over his chain.

'The one and only Ali Pali!' bellowed Benny. 'Mr Spello himself!'

Ali waved and beamed. He was popular with the crowd, most of whom owned spellovisions. If it wasn't for him they would spend every night staring at a blank screen.

'And a big hand for our Mystery Celebrities!' announced Benny. 'I give you Scott Sinister, star of stage and screen!'

'Hooray!' bellowed the fans of the *Killer Poodle* movies. Scott sucked his cheeks in and acknowledged the applause with a gracious nod.

'Give it up for Luscious Lulu Lamarre, boys and girls!'

'Hooray!' came the enthusiastic response. Well, everyone loves a bit of glamour. Lulu simpered and pouted while cameras flashed and the Vampire cameraman moved in for a close-up. All the females in the audience took in the details of her evening gown and vowed to save up for the next ten years, then go out and buy one just like it.

'And last but not lea— well, let's give him a big hand anyway – the Mayor of Sludeghaven!'

Nobody cheered. Somebody shouted, 'Tell him to sort the drains out!' and there were a couple of boos, but apart from that, the Mayor was greeted by stony silence, which was a bit sad but there you go.

'So,' went on Benny, 'while the judges take their seats, I'll go ahead and introduce the first band. They're mean, they're keen and they're hoping to make a BIG impression. All the way from – er –' Benny consulted his clipboard – 'Under A Bridge Somewhere – I give you *One Big Troll and Some Other Biggish Ones!*'

'UH! UH! UH!' went up the cry from the Troll

fans in the audience. Being Trolls, they didn't have banners with writing on, but most of them had brought a collection of stones to bang together to show their support, so they certainly made their presence felt.

DJ Benny scuttled off and *One Big Troll and Some Other Biggish Ones* lumbered onstage. Each carried a large rock under one arm and was swinging an iron club hammer. They stood in an uneven line and faced the audience. One Big Troll carefully adjusted the mike. Then they all raised their hammers and proceeded to thump the rocks. There was no attention to timing. They just thumped away, as and when they felt like it. *Clang! Bong! Dong!* It was music to Trollish ears, but to everyone else it just sounded like rocks being hammered.

'Oh.' At the judging table, Lulu paused in applying more lipstick and made a face. 'A percussion band. How very boring.'

'Nothing wrong with percussion,' said Scott. Actually, there was a *lot* wrong with percussion the way the Trolls played it, but Scott had a game plan. He had decided that whatever Lulu said, he would say the opposite.

The Mayor reached for the water jug, then noticed that nobody had provided him with a glass. There wasn't a cushion on his chair either, so his chin rested on the table.

The rock thumping went on for quite some time. Eventually, Benny Bonkers called a halt by marching onstage and grabbing the microphone. The Trolls clanged and bonged to a halt and stood panting heavily.

'Well done, lads,' said Benny. 'That was a number entitled – er –' he consulted his clipboard – ' "We Will Bang Some Rocks At You". That's a translation, of course. In Trollish, it's known as "Uh Uh Uh Uh Uh Uh Uh". Hope I pronounced that right?' He raised an eyebrow at the perspiring Trolls, who all nodded and said, 'UH.'

'So,' said Benny. 'Over to our judges. Comments, please?'

'Dreadful,' said Lulu. 'Complete and utter twaddle.'

'Wonderful,' said Scott. 'Passion, commitment, it has it all.'

'Ah,' said Benny. 'We have a slight disagreement. Mr Mayor?'

'Well,' said the Mayor. 'As Mayor, I –'

'Sorry, we're pressed for time. Ali? Your thoughts?'

'Interesting,' said Ali. 'Limited appeal, I suspect, but – interesting.'

'Well, there you have it. All right, lads, you can get

offstage. Moving on now to the next act. They're pink, they're pretty and they're into ponds. Who could I be talking about but – *The Gnomettes!*'

The crowd roared good-natured approval as *The Gnomettes* tripped on, trying not to collide with *One Big Troll and Some Other Biggish Ones* who were clumping offstage with their rocks, looking quite cheerful despite mixed reviews.

'Well, they're certainly pretty,' remarked Scott loudly, for Lulu's benefit. '*Very* pretty. Unlike some I could mention.'

Lulu reached over and tipped the jug of water into his lap.

The Gnomettes gathered round the microphone, simpered, fluffed out their dresses and burst into song.

> '*Down at the pond there are tiddlers,*
> *Minnows and sticklebacks tooooooo,*
> *But we go fishing for compliments,*
> *That's what we like to doooooooooo . . .*'

O'Brian sat in the van, hugging his Pot and staring at Gareth. Gareth stared back. He knew O'Brian didn't want to talk right now. Everything that had to be said had been said. Fate would take its course.

The door opened and Filth climbed in, followed by Tallula and Arthur.

'Hey,' said Filth. 'What's up, man?'

'Nothing,' said O'Brian.

'Don't you want to come and listen to the competition?' asked Arthur. 'It's rubbish so far.'

'No,' said O'Brian. 'Leave me alone.'

A little silence fell. Filth tapped out a rhythm on the dashboard.

'Well, you can't stay here for ever,' said Arthur after a bit. 'You've got a solo to play, remember? That nice little riff you worked out after Tallula's first verse. Right?'

'I'm not playing. You'll have to go on without me. I'm not in the mood.'

'Not in the *mood*,' repeated Arthur. 'I see. I don't suppose – this is just a wild guess, mind – but I don't suppose this has anything to do with you being *cursed by a Fairy*?'

O'Brian looked up sharply. His shocked eyes travelled from one face to another, finally resting on Tallula.

'I told them,' said Tallula. 'I heard you talking to Gareth. I was in the back trying to sleep. Sorry. I thought it'd help to get things out in the open.'

'Why didn't you say, man?' asked Filth. 'That's some heavy guilt trip you've been on.'

172

'Right,' agreed Arthur. 'We're your friends, after all.'

'You won't be, though,' said O'Brian bitterly. 'Not when we lose.'

'Lose?' Filth was amazed. 'Why would we lose? We're *good.*'

'I know that. But don't you see? I'll be dragging my bad luck onstage with me and it'll rub off on *you.* If I play, we don't stand a chance.'

'We'll take that risk,' said Arthur. 'We're *The Witchway Rhythm Boys.* Sorry, Tallula, I mean *The Witchway Rhythm Boys and a Werewolf Girl.* We play together or we don't play at all.'

'Yeah,' said Filth. 'We need that solo, dude. And it's not about winning or losing. It's about playing.'

'That's easy for you to say. You get all the fan mail and look good in your T-shirt. I'm just a figure of fun. Look, I'm *sorry,* all right? I'm sorry I've mucked things up. But I'm not going on and that's that.'

'Right,' said Arthur. 'That's it. You won't listen to us, so I'm calling in reinforcements. Come on, you two. Let's go and get TT.'

Chapter Twenty

The Battle Continues

'*Fishing, fishing, we like to go fishing,*
   Fishing for complimeeeeeeeents!'

The final note died away and the Gnome contingent in the audience burst into loud applause. *The Gnomettes* curtsied and looked pleased with themselves as Benny Bonkers ran to the microphone.

'And that's it from the lovely *Gnomettes*. Comments from the judges? Ali?'

'Interesting,' said Ali. 'Fish-based, but – interesting.'

'Thank you, Ali. Mr Mayor?'

'Well, as Mayor –'

'Keep it short, please. Time's pressing.'

'Yes, well, as Mayor –'

'Lulu? What about you?'

'Appalling,' sniffed Lulu. 'Tuneless and time-wasting and they don't suit pink.'

The Gnomettes stopped smiling and looked highly put out.

'Oh dear,' said Benny sadly. 'Not too encouraging there I'm afraid, ladies. Scott?'

'Charming,' said Scott. 'Lovely ladies, lovely song. A breath of fresh air compared to the claptrap that passes for music in certain shows these days. In fact, I'd like to hear it again.'

'No time for encores, Scott,' said Benny. 'Right, girls, off you go. Next up is an act I know all you Zombie fans have been waiting for. It's *Betty and the Bully Girls* singing a catchy little number entitled "Get You In The Playground".'

'I wish they'd get *you* in the playground,' hissed Lulu, pointing her sharpened pencil at Scott, who snatched it, broke it in two and dropped both halves in her water glass. The spellovision camera moved in for a close-up, and they hastily put on smiles.

Meanwhile, backstage, Arthur, Filth and Tallula were in deep consultation with TT and Chip. The other bands were staring curiously, aware that there was some sort of crisis. *One Big Troll and Some Other Biggish Ones* were wiping their rocks and putting them into a big sack. They had done their bit, of course, and so had *The Gnomettes*, who were clustered round the tea urn. *Rodney and the Rattles* stood in a corner with their backs to everyone, tuning up their banjos and sneering.

'Really?' said TT. 'Cursed by a Fairy? Well, that's explains a lot. You'd think he'd have mentioned it.'

'Too embarrassed,' said Arthur. 'He's pretty upset. Says he's lost his Leprechaun Luck and won't play.'

'Of course he's playing,' said TT. 'All right, you don't mess with Fairies, everyone knows that. But he's got to go on. He's in the band.'

'We know,' said Arthur. 'We've told him that. But he thinks he'll make us lose.'

'I'll go out and have a word – he'll listen to me. It's called crisis management. Somebody get him some tea. The urn's working now. Chip, you come with me.'

'We'll get you in the playground, playground, playground,
We'll get you in the playground and try to make you cry!'

Betty and the Bully Girls were giving it their all. It was a horrible tune with horrible words and they performed it horribly, with actions. The Zombies in the audience were loving it but everyone else looked a bit scared, as well they might.

'We'll throw away your lunchbox, lunchbox, lunchbox,
We'll throw away your lunchbox and poke you in the eye!
Shoobee doo, shoobee dum, pull your hair, kick your bum,
We'll get you in the playground and try to make you cry!'

To most people's relief, the song ended there. Betty strode around the stage flexing her biceps and one of the *Bully Girls* kicked over the microphone stand.

'Well, there we have it,' cried Benny, zooming on. 'A tough message from Betty and the girls. Comments, judges, please. Mr Mayor?'

'Well, as Mayor, I –'

'Moving swiftly on. Ali?'

'Interesting. A little *fierce* perhaps, but – interesting.'

'What about you, Scott?'

'Hated it,' said Scott with a shudder. 'Complete rubbish from start to finish.'

'Come up here and say that,' offered Betty, hands on hips.

'He wouldn't dare,' said Lulu. 'He's even scared of little poodle puppies. Personally, I absolutely *adored* it.'

*

'Here he is!' announced TT, marching cheerfully into the tent. He was followed by Chip, who had O'Brian slung over his shoulder like a sack of potatoes. 'Just a few last-minute nerves. I've given him a little pep talk. He's feeling much better now. Put him down, Chip – he's fine.'

'No, I'm not,' muttered O'Brian, slithering to the floor. He accepted the paper cup of weak tea that Tallula thrust into his hand, though. He needed it after the pep talk, which consisted of being forcibly ejected from the van and carted across the car park by Chip while TT shouted things about loyalty and teamwork in his ear.

'Shall I hold your Pot for you?' offered Tallula gently.

'No thanks. I can manage.'

'That's right, you get that tea down you,' instructed TT. 'The rest of us'll start unloading the van.'

O'Brian found himself alone. Balancing the tea on the Pot, he made his way to a quiet spot and hunkered down with his back to the canvas. He kept his eyes lowered but was aware of whispers and muffled titters from the other bands.

A shadow fell over him. He looked up and found himself staring into a pair of dark glasses.

'What's in the pot, little man?' sneered Rodney. '*Do* tell. We're all curious.'

'Wouldn't you like to know?' snapped O'Brian.

'Well – *obviously*. That's why I'm asking.'

'None of your business,' said O'Brian shortly.

'What do you call that hanging round your neck?' sneered Rodney. 'Some sort of *instrument*? Or a piece of bathroom plumbing?'

'It's a penny whistle, if you must know.'

'Oh, I *see*! And that's traditional with you Pixies, is it? Hear that, lads? The Pixie's playing a pen—'

'What did you just call me?'

'What?'

'Did you just call me a Pixie?'

'Yes. So?'

And O'Brian exploded. He leapt to his feet, sending the Pot rolling away under the no-food table.

'Similar hats! We wear *similar hats*! I'm a *Leprechaun*, bone brain! A Leprechaun and proud of it! Call me a Pixie again! Come on, say it again!'

At that point, *Betty and the Bully Girls* came clumping in, fresh from their spot in the limelight. The general reaction to their efforts had been negative apart from Lulu, and even she had sounded insincere. However, they brightened up at the prospect of a fight.

'Are you *threatening* me?' sneered Rodney. But he backed away. He was wearing a white suit. The

Leprechaun had a cup of tea in his hand. There was a distinct danger of spillage.

'Hey – hey!' TT's alarmed voice came from the tent entrance. 'What's going on?'

The others stood behind him. Tallula and Filth were carrying drums and Chip had Arthur's piano on his back.

'He called me a Pixie!' roared O'Brian. The T-shirt was constricting him, but that only made him madder. He drew back his arm, ready to hurl the tea over Rodney's pristine white jacket. Luckily, at that moment, Benny Bonkers came bustling in.

'What's happening here? Everyone's waiting! Come on, Rodney, you're on!'

With relief, *Rodney and the Rattles* hurriedly picked up their banjos and made for the stage, leaving O'Brian dancing on the spot, puce with rage.

'Hey man, cool it,' soothed Filth. 'He's not worth it, dude.'

'He called me a Pixie!'

'Yeah, yeah. Don't let it get to you.'

'Quite right,' said TT. 'He's just trying to unsettle you. You should rise above it. Right, Arthur?'

'Right,' agreed Arthur. And Tallula stooped down and gave O'Brian a comforting little hug. O'Brian resisted for a moment, then gave in.

'All right,' he said. 'He got to me, that's all. I'm OK now.'

'That's the spirit,' said Arthur. 'Just drink up your tea and relax, because we're on next.'

'All right. Where's my Pot?'

'I don't know,' said Arthur. 'You had it when we left.'

'I think it rolled under the table,' said O'Brian. Everyone looked under the table. There was a sea of crumpled paper cups and the odd trampled sandwich.

But no Pot.

'*NOOOOOOOOOOOOO!*' The anguished scream burst from O'Brian's lips. Everyone covered their ears.

Chapter Twenty-One
We're On!

'And now,' Benny Bonkers told the audience, 'the act I know all you Skeletons have been waiting for. It's *Rodney and the Rattles*!'

There was a bit of scattered applause as Rodney came swaggering onstage, followed by *the Rattles*. The area at the front of the stage had thinned out. The sun was really hot now. An ice-cream van had arrived in the field and most people apart from a handful of Skeletons had joined the queue.

'Handsome,' cooed Lulu. 'Such lovely suits.'

'Posers,' sniffed Scott.

TWAAANNNG! The Rattles struck a chord. Rodney stepped up to the mike, sneered, then burst into song. He had a high, nasal singing voice that grated on the ear.

'Everything's all about meeee,' sang Rodney.
'I'm handsome as can beeee,
I look so cool in my white suit
As everyone must agreeeee . . .'

TWANG! TWONG! went the banjos.

'The girls all faint and sigh
Whenever I'm passing by,
They'd like to be my girlfriend
But none of them qualify . . .'

'It's gone!' wailed O'Brian. 'I just put it down for two minutes – two minutes, that's all – and it's vanished!'

'Cool it, man,' said Filth. 'It probably just, like, carried on rolling. It'll be in a corner somewhere.'

'Or maybe someone's hidden it for a joke,' suggested TT.

'A joke?' shrieked O'Brian. 'A *joke*? You're saying this is *funny*?'

'I'm saying it's just temporarily mislaid. Keep your voice down – everyone's looking.'

Indeed, everyone was. Clearly there was yet another drama unfolding.

'What's up with the nutter?' enquired one of the Bully Girls.

'Nothing,' said Arthur. 'It's a private matter. He's fine.'

'No, I'm not!'

'Calm *down*. We'll have another look. As soon as we get offstage.'

'I'm not going onstage. Not without my Pot.'

'Oh yes, you are,' said Tallula, coming up from behind. She had made three searches of the tent, although it was clearly pointless.

'I'm not so.'

'You *are*. Look, I'm sorry if I sound unsympathetic, but we've all got problems, you know. Arthur's homesick, I've got to go out in public wearing this horrible frock and Filth – well, I'm sure he's got worries too, haven't you, Filth?'

Filth shrugged. 'Not really,' he said. 'Just looking forward to the gig, you know?'

'Which is worse?' went on Tallula. 'Losing a pot of gold which you don't ever open or letting your friends down? Will you just forget about everything else and do what you're supposed to do, which is *play*? And don't start whining about the curse because we've been through all that. It's not all about you. It's about Crash 'n' Bang. This is our big chance. *Are you going to ruin it?*'

Everyone stared at O'Brian. He fingered the neck of his T-shirt. Then, slowly, he picked up the whistle.

'No,' he said. 'I'm not. To heck with it. You can count me in.' Which was just as well, because right at that moment, Benny Bonkers came running with *Rodney and the Rattles* strutting along behind.

'Where are *The Witchway Rhythm Boys?*' he shouted. 'Come on, lads, get your instruments onstage! You're on!'

'Is this the last band?' yawned Lulu. 'Because I'm bored now.'

'Really?' said Scott. 'Personally, I'm thoroughly enjoying myself. What about you, Mr Mayor?'

'Well, as Mayor –'

'Ali?' interrupted Lulu. 'Is this the last band?'

'It is,' said Ali. '*The Witchway Rhythm Boys.*'

'Oh, right,' said Scott. 'That funny little outfit from Witchway Wood. I've heard them before. Nothing special.'

'So have I,' said Lulu. 'The drummer's adorable. There he is, look. *Sweeeet.*'

Up on the stage, a small Fiend was unhurriedly setting up his drum kit. A short, squat Troll was stomping around with a piano on his back while a fussy-looking Dragon decided the best place to put it. A Leprechaun wearing an odd, pink, lumpy T-shirt that was clearly unbearably tight was hanging around in the background, together with –

'Oh my!' said Lulu. 'A Werewolf! Is she going to *sing*? What a horrible frock.'

'It's not a horr—' began Scott, then stopped. Even he had to admit that the frock was indeed horrible. He tried to think of something nice to say about the unexpected Werewolf but couldn't come up with anything.

'As Mayor,' said the Mayor firmly, determined to get a word in for once. 'As *Mayor*, I must say I shall be glad when this is over. It seems to be getting rather chilly, do you notice?'

And it was. Overhead, clouds were gathering. The crowds were uneasily peering up at the sky, reaching for rugs to put round their shoulders. This was all wrong. The sun always shone in Sludgehaven. Clouds were unheard of at this time of year. Little white, friendly, fluffy ones, maybe – but not big, black, boiling, angry ones.

Benny Bonkers hurried onstage looking anxious.

'Ready, boys?' he asked. 'Because time's getting on.'

'Oh yeah,' said Filth with a grin. 'We're ready. Bring it on.'

'Right, boys and girls!' declaimed Benny into the mike. 'Here we go with the last band. All the way from Witchway Wood, we have *The Witchway Rhythm Boys!* Give 'em a big hand!' And he ran offstage.

But the crowd had lost interest in the stage. Nobody clapped. Nobody cheered. Everybody was staring up at the darkening sky. A strange silence had spread across the field. It seemed that everyone was holding their breath, waiting for something. The only sound was the distant chimes of the hastily retreating ice-cream van.

Filth picked up his drumsticks. Arthur raised his claws over the keyboard. O'Brian put his whistle to his mouth. Tallula walked to the microphone, straightened her shoulders and took a shaky breath. In the wings, TT and Chip crossed their fingers . . .

CRRRRRRRAAAAACK!

A mighty clap of thunder rent the heavens, accompanied by a flash of lightning –

And then came the rain! Although the word *rain* isn't strong enough for what it actually did. It deluged. It poured. It spouted, bucketed, pelted, came down in sheets, blankets and extra-thick duvets! Nothing can describe how hard it rained.

Within seconds, the grassy field was a mudbath. Puddles formed and joined up with each other. The crowd turned their backs on the stage and began pushing and shoving and splashing their way over the slippery ground towards the gates like a stampede of wildebeests in soggy sunhats. The judging panel deserted their table and fled towards the shelter of the Celebrity Tent which, being flimsy as well as glittery, promptly collapsed on top of them.

The Boys hesitated. The stage was open to the elements. It was already covered with a slick of water. Rain hammered down on their heads and on their instruments. Their Moonmad T-shirts were dishcloths. Tallula's hair was a bedraggled mess. Rain filled their eyes, flooded their ears and streamed off their noses. But – this was their moment. Nothing was going to take it away from them.

'A one!' shouted Arthur.

'A two!' yelled O'Brian.

'A one, two, three!' shrieked Filth.

And they began to play.

My, did they play! They played better than they had ever played in their lives. This was Crash 'n' Bang and it crashed and banged like nothing you've ever heard before. It was fire, it was sparks, it was excitement. It rose above the sound of the rain and it exploded! The drums smashed, the piano rumbled, the penny whistle twinkled and soared. And then, to add to the glory of it all – Tallula sang.

> '*I used to be a loner,*
> *I used to be a freak,*
> *I used to be a moaner,*
> *I used to be a geek . . .*'

TT hurtled on to the stage. He just couldn't help it. He stood with his arms outstretched, swaying in time.

'Yeah!' he shouted. 'Crash 'n' Bang! Yeeeeeaaah!'

> *'But since I started singing,*
> *My life has changed and how!*
> *I used to be a Werewolf but I'm all right now.'*

Chip was onstage now, eyes ablaze, jigging from side to side with his knuckles rapping the floor.

'UH!' he roared. 'UH, UH, UH!'

> *'I'm all right noooooooow!*
> *Yes, I'm all right noooooooow!*
> *I can growl, I can bite,*
> *But I can sing, so that's all right,*
> *Used to be a Werewolf but I'm*
> *All right now! Take it away, boys!'*

And the Boys took it away. They took it away further than they had ever taken it before. Arthur forgot about all the little annoyances he had endured over the course of the last week. O'Brian forgot about the curse. Tallula forgot about her frock. And Filth? Well, he only cared about his drums anyway.

It didn't matter that it was raining. It didn't matter

that they were playing to a deserted field. It didn't matter that there was no one to judge them. All that mattered was the music – the tightness of the drum rhythms, the perfection of the piano chords, the magical interweaving of the penny whistle. Crash 'n' Bang. That was what mattered.

But, wait. A deserted field? Let's look again.

Standing right before the stage was a ragbag collection of – what – *fans*?

Yes. Fans. Friends, family, supporters. All swaying and grinning and tapping their feet, holding umbrellas and waving a huge banner. The letters were running badly but you could still read them.

GO BOYS! WE'RE WITH YOU!

Who are they, these lovely supporters who had organised a coach to bring them all the way to Sludgehaven to spring such a wonderful surprise? I will tell you.

Sludgegooey. Charlene, Jemella and Roxanne. Arthur's mum. O'Brian's fourteen brothers. Spag Yeti. Conf Yeti. Chip's cousin Rocky, who he hadn't seen in years. Helpful Bob. TT's Aunty Maureen, who had given him Gareth. Even Tallula's Werewolf friend Shirley, who she had lost touch with after the hairbrush row. And there was one other.

Standing slap bang in the middle of the line was a Fairy. A Fairy with delicate little wings and a gauzy dress. In her hand was a tiny wand that she waved in time to the music. Over the gauzy dress, she wore a little leather jacket with holes cut for her wings. On her dainty feet were galumphing great boots that you would never associate with Fairies. It just goes to show. You shouldn't make assumptions. Fairies *do* like Crash 'n' Bang. Well, this one did.

Incredible though all this was, the Boys didn't let it put them off their stroke. And Tallula didn't let the sight of Shirley faze her. She had another verse to sing.

'I used to be a loner,
I used to be a nerd,
An always-stay-at-homer,
Who never said a word,
But since I started singing,
My life has changed and how,
Yes, I used to be a Werewolf
But I'm all right now!
I'm all right noooooooow!

Yes, I'm all right noooooooow!
I can growl, I can bite,
But I can sing, so that's all right,

Used to be a Werewolf but I'm
A-l-l-l-l-l-lll
Ri-i-i-i-ght
NOOOOOOOOOOWWWWWW!

Tallula's final triumphant howl died away, Filth threw his drumsticks in the air, Arthur slammed down the piano lid and O'Brian kissed his penny whistle and let it fall back to his chest. Then, reluctantly, he faced the Fairy.

She gave him a knowing wink. It was a 'you've-suffered-enough-and-have-hopefully-learned-your-lesson-but-cross-me-again-at-your-peril' sort of wink.

O'Brian winked back. It was a rueful 'I-know-I-overstepped-the-mark-but-I'm-truly-sorry-and-glad-you-liked-the-music' sort of wink.

Then – very deliberately – the Fairy raised her wand . . . and the rain stopped! It didn't die out slowly – it just cut off. The sun came swimming out from behind the clouds as though it had never been away, blazing and shining and glistening in the steaming puddles, making the world a truly wonderful place again.

Now, what could be nicer than that?

Chapter Twenty-Two
Going Home

A huge moon swam in the sky as the band van drove slowly up the winding trail leading to the top of the Misty Mountains. It was overheating a bit because TT had forgotten to top up the water. Steam was rising from the bonnet and the engine was making a funny noise.

'We'll stop for a few minutes,' said TT. 'Let it cool off.'

He turned off the engine and applied the handbrake.

Everyone sat quietly, looking back over their shoulders at the faraway lights of distant Sludgehaven. Well, everyone except Tallula, who didn't have a window.

'I'll try the radio,' said Filth. He reached out

and fiddled with the knobs. A silky voice filled the interior.

'. . . *and this is, of course, Sylvester Smoothy, bringing you* Sounds Of The Night. *Before the next request, a bit of disappointing news. We were hoping to announce the winner of today's Battle of the Bands competition, but an unexpected cloudburst meant that the competition ended in a washout. We tried contacting Ali Pali, but he was unavailable. Rumour has it that he is having second thoughts about his new record label and thinking about taking a long holiday instead. Neither Scott Sinister nor Lulu Lamarre were contactable, but I have here the Mayor of Sludgehaven, who would like to say —'*

The radio crackled horribly then lapsed into silence.

'Lost the reception again,' said Filth and switched it off.

Nobody said anything for a while. They just watched the faraway lights.

'Well,' said Arthur. 'It's over. That's it. We played in a battle that nobody won. But d'you know what? I'm not that bothered. I never really cared about the fame and riches bit. And I wouldn't want to go touring anyway because of Mam.'

'Yeah,' said Filth. 'I just wanted to play Crash 'n' Bang in public, that's all. Just once, to see what it felt like. And we did. And it was great. But I'm ready for home now. Gotta clean that kitchen, man.'

'It went down surprisingly well with the fans, didn't it?' said TT. 'I couldn't believe it when they all turned up. I honestly think some of them actually *liked* it. My Aunty Maureen was very complimentary. Fancy her showing up. Gareth liked seeing her again, didn't you, Gareth?'

Gareth blew a bubble to show that he had.

There had indeed been a happy mingling when the Boys and Tallula had stepped offstage. There had been hugging and much congratulation and pats on the back. There had been a few awkward moments as well, of course. O'Brian and the Fairy weren't too sure how to act with each other but finally decided on a stiff handshake and an assurance from O'Brian that, in the future, shoes would be mended on time, on the house. O'Brian's brothers had been on the Fairy's side, but O'Brian didn't feel too resentful because at least they had turned up to support him and pretended to enjoy the music. Besides, he was curse-free! Not only had the missing Pot turned up in the back of the van – why or how it came to be there will for ever remain a mystery – but even better, the T-shirt had returned to normal size so that he was able to get it off! He had presented it to

TT, who used it to wipe the dead flies off the van's windscreen.

Tallula and Shirley had given each other a hairy hug and promised to go clothes shopping some time. Arthur's mother had brought him a home-made curry, so he was happy. Sludgegooey hadn't bothered to bring Filth anything, but the Banshees had baked him a special cake with his name on so it didn't matter. Helpful Bob had smilingly thrust an envelope in TT's hand, which turned out to be a very, *very* large bill. Interest on the Magic Card. That was a bit of a downer. Even the reunion with his Aunty Maureen wasn't stopping TT worrying about how he was going to pay, now that there would be no cheque and no foreseeable future with *Genie Sounds*. Unless . . .

'O'Brian,' said TT. 'You know that Pot Of Gold?'

'Yes?' said O'Brian. The Pot was rolling about in the back somewhere. It was wonderful not to have it in his lap.

'You know how you were saying you don't actually *spend* it?'

'Yes.'

'Well – er – how would you feel about giving me some? I've got a bit of a cash-flow problem.'

'I don't see why not,' said O'Brian easily. 'There's more to life than gold.'

'Never thought I'd hear those words coming from the lips of a Leprechaun,' said Arthur.

'But he's a Crash 'n' Bang Leprechaun,' said Tallula, from the back. 'That's different.'

'That's right,' said O'Brian happily. 'I am.' He didn't mention that one of the features of a Leprechaun Pot is that it never empties. However much you dip into it, it just fills up again. But he kept quiet about that because it wouldn't make him seem so generous.

'Thanks, O'Brian,' said TT. 'Hope you didn't mind my asking.'

'Oh no,' said O'Brian. 'Not a bit of it. Always happy to help a friend in need.'

TT gave a little sigh. 'Glad you still think of me as a friend.'

'Why wouldn't we?' asked Tallula.

'Well – things didn't work out that well. We're not going to be millionaires. I guess I'm not cut out to be a manager after all.'

'Hey, man,' said Filth. 'You did OK, dude.'

'Of course you did,' said Tallula. 'We wouldn't be here now if it wasn't for you. Right, Arthur?'

'You did fine,' said Arthur. 'All right, so we won't be rich and famous, but it was an experience. Not that I want another one in a hurry, but it'll be something to remember, won't it? When we're playing at the Zombie Reunion Dance next Saturday.'

'But I cancelled it,' TT reminded him.

'So un-cancel it. You're the manager now. You'd better warn them that we'll be slipping in a Crash 'n' Bang number or two. They'll argue at first, but they'll just have to put up with it. They might even end up liking it.'

'What about you, Tallula?' asked Filth. 'Free to sing next Saturday?'

'Try and stop me,' said Tallula happily.

'UH?' chipped in Chip. He was looking a bit anxious. 'Uh-uh-UH?'

'Yeah, dude,' said Filth. 'Of course you're still the roadie.'

'The engine's cooled a bit,' said TT. 'If we take it steady, we should make it to that old Hobgoblin's filling station. Top up with petrol and water. Maybe get a few of those egg rolls, eh? Should keep us going until we get home.'

And so they went home to Witchway Wood. It took hours but nobody minded because they had a lot to talk about. Arthur's complaints about the egg rolls took up at least an hour. And there was always I Spy.

When they reached the mountain where Tallula

lived, she asked to be dropped off by the side of the trail. There were hugs all round and a promise to meet up for rehearsal next Wednesday. Then she loped off into the trees. The others watched her go.

'She'll be going for a run and a bit of a howl,' said TT, adding hastily, 'Nothing wrong with that.'

'Think she'll be all right?' asked O'Brian.

'Yeah,' said Filth. 'She's used to being a Werewolf –'

'And she's all right noooooowwwwww!' chorused the others. Well, Chip said 'UH!' and Gareth blew a stream of bubbles – but they meant the same thing.

So. The End. It always arrives so quickly, doesn't it?

TOO quickly in our opinion and so we've decided to give you a few extra pages of fun and laughter.

Do you want to know:

 where Kaye Umansky gets the ideas for her writing?

 how to keep up to speed with all the news from Witchway Wood?

 what Crash 'n' Bang music REALLY sounds like?

some side-splittingly funny Crash 'n' Bang gags?

how one of our favourite books by the wonderful Kaye Umansky starts?

We thought so!

Turn over the page and all will be revealed . . .

For more puzzles, recipes and spells to try, go to
www.pongwiffy.com

Meet Kaye

Q: So, Kaye, can you describe yourself in 5 words?
A: Large, loud, friendly, cat-loving snow-lover.

Q: And how did you become a writer?
A: As a kid, I was a big reader. Other writers' books inspired me to have a go myself. It was a hobby for years - I didn't think of trying to get published until I was really ancient (40).

Q: Where do you write your books?
A: In my tiny blue office upstairs. It has stars that light up in the ceiling, lots of fairy lights and loads of mobiles, photos, books, and bits and pieces, including a witch's hat, broomstick and cauldron. Children's letters and drawings are displayed on the walls. I love it up there.

Q: What do you do when you're not writing books?
A: I think about the next one. I read, watch telly, listen to music and eat all the lovely food my husband cooks.

Q: Do you have a favourite Witchway Wood character?
A: I love 'em all. But I think TT (the Thing in the Moonmad T-shirt) really comes into his own in Crash 'N' Bang. Band manager is the best job he's ever had. I like his enthusiasm.

Find out more about Kaye at: www.kayeumansky.com

For some witchy wit, Troll chuckles and Leprechaun laughs, try these howlers on your friends (not to mention your fiends):

Where are Troll films made?
Trollywood

What is Trolls' favourite music?
Hard Rock Music

What do you call a Leprechaun with a bad haircut?
Shaun

What do all Giants have in common?
Really big feet

Why did the Gnome cross the road?
Because he didn't Gno what was on the other side

Why did the twin Witches find it so hard to make friends?
Because no one knew which Witch was which

Why do Dragons hate school?
Because the lessons just Drag-on and on and on . . .

CHAPTER ONE

Entertaining

'Witch Sharkadder! My old friend!' cried Witch Pongwiffy, opening the front boulder with her very best welcoming smile firmly fixed in place. 'What a lovely surprise. Welcome to my humble cave. My, you do look nice. Is that a new hairdo, or have you had some sort of terrible shock, ha ha? Just my little joke. Come in, come in. Let me take your hat.'

She seized the tall hat, gave it a respectful little brush and waited until Sharkadder's back was turned before booting it into a dark corner.

'It's hardly a surprise if you knew I was coming,' remarked Sharkadder coldly, advancing into the cave. 'I know you want to be my friend again, Pongwiffy, but

I'm not at all sure I want to be yours. So stop sucking up.'

There was no doubt that Pongwiffy was being revoltingly smarmy – but it was for a good reason. She and Sharkadder were usually best friends, but they had recently had one of their quarrels, and Pongwiffy was anxious to make amends.

'Oh, you're not still thinking about that silly old quarrel, are you? Come on, Sharky, let bygones be bygones. Have a look at my new cave. I only moved in last week. You're my first guest.'

Sharkadder stared around distastefully.

Pongwiffy's cave wasn't a pleasant sight. It had shocking damp problems for a start. Slimy green moss grew on the walls, and the floor was a sea of muddy puddles. The broken-down furniture wasn't so much arranged as thrown in any old how. Thick black steam belched from the horrible-looking slop which bubbled and heaved in the cauldron.

'Well, sit down, Sharky. Make yourself at home,' fussed Pongwiffy, removing Sharkadder's cloak and dropping it into a slimy pool.

'There's nowhere to sit,' observed Sharkadder.

'You'll have to use that cardboard box. I haven't sorted out the chairs yet. That's the trouble when you've just moved in. It takes ages to get organised, doesn't it?'

'You've never been organised,' said Sharkadder. 'What's that terrible stink? Smells like skunk.'

'It is,' said Pongwiffy cheerfully. 'It's tonight's supper. My speciality. You'll love it. Skunk stew. I'll just give it a stir.' And she took a large ladle and poked at the gurgling goo in the cauldron.

'Oh,' said Sharkadder, wishing she'd stayed at home. 'Skunk stew. Really?'

'I knew you'd be pleased,' said Pongwiffy. 'Now, tell me truthfully. How do you like the cave? It's a little damp, I know, and perhaps a bit small, but it was very cheap. Of course, it's a nuisance being in Goblin Territory, but I can't afford anything better at the moment. What do you think of it?'

'It's a dump,' said Sharkadder. 'It's a smelly little slum. It's not fit to live in. It's squalid and yucky. It's the worst cave I've ever been in. It suits you.'

'It does,' agreed Pongwiffy, pleased. 'I feel it's me. It's a pity about the Goblins, though. I'll tell you about them later. Now then. How much stew for you, Sharky?'

'Er – about half a teaspoon,' said Sharkadder hastily. 'I had a huge lunch. And I think I've got a touch of tummy trouble.'

'Nonsense,' said Pongwiffy, relentlessly approaching with a huge, greasy plateful. 'Get that down you. That's a lovely perfume you're wearing. Don't tell me

– let me guess. "Night In A Fish Factory", right? And I do so like the new hairstyle. It really suits you. Brings out the beakiness of your nose.'

'It does, doesn't it?' agreed Sharkadder, finally coming round after such an onslaught of flattery. She scrabbled in her bag, took out a small, cracked hand mirror and examined the frazzled mess with satisfaction.

'I've got some new hair rollers,' she explained. 'Little hedgehogs. You warm them up. Not too much, or they get bad-tempered and nip. Just enough to send them to sleep. Then you wind the hair round, and wait for them to cool. And it comes out all curly, like this.'

'Beautiful,' nodded Pongwiffy through a mouthful of stew. 'You always look so nice, Sharky. I don't know how you do it.'

'Yes, well, I do try to take care of myself,' said Sharkadder, tossing her tangles and applying sickly green lipstick. 'You'd look a lot better yourself if you washed once in a while. And changed that disgusting old cardigan.'

'What's wrong with my cardigan?' asked Pongwiffy, clutching the offending garment to her bony chest.

'What's right with it? It's got holes. It's got no buttons. You've spilt so much food down it, you can hardly see the pattern. It looks like it's been knitted

with congealed egg. Want me to go on?'

'No,' muttered Pongwiffy sulkily.

But it was true. Pongwiffy's sense of personal hygiene left a lot to be desired.

'As for those flies that buzz around you all day long, it's time you swatted them,' added Sharkadder, enjoying herself.

'Swat Buzz and Dave? Never!' declared Pongwiffy, aghast at the idea. She was fond of her flies. They circled round her hat, shared her food, and slept on her pillow at night.

'Look, let's not talk about flies and cardigans. You'll never change me, Sharky. I like the way I am. Try some stew. I made it specially.'

'I can't. I haven't got a spoon,' hedged Sharkadder.

'What on earth do you need a spoon for? Slurp it from the plate, like I'm doing,' said Pongwiffy, demonstrating.

'No, I want a spoon,' insisted Sharkadder.

Pongwiffy sighed and went to the sink. Sharkadder watched her crawl under the table, duck under the cobwebs, heave a heavy wardrobe to one side and kick a dozen cardboard boxes out of the way.

'I don't know how you bear it,' said Sharkadder with a shudder. 'Don't you ever tidy up?'

'Nope,' said Pongwiffy truthfully, returning with a spoon.

Sharkadder eyed it with a critical frown. 'It's dirty,' she observed. 'What's all this crusty stuff?'

'Last week's skunk stew,' explained Pongwiffy. 'No point in washing it, seeing as we're having the same. Now, what was I going to tell you? Oh yes. My new neighbours. You see . . .'

'I want a clean spoon,' interrupted Sharkadder.

The strain of being a polite hostess was suddenly more than Pongwiffy could bear.

'Honestly!' she shouted. 'You're such a fusspot sometimes. I go to all the trouble of inviting you for supper, and all you do is . . .'

Just at that moment, there came an interruption. There was an ear-splitting crash, and the walls shook. The Goblins in the cave next door had arrived home. You should know quite a bit about the Goblins Next Door, because they feature rather a lot in this story.

The Goblins Next Door consisted of a whole Gaggle. A Gaggle is seven Goblins. These were called Plugugly, Stinkwart, Eyesore, Slopbucket, Sproggit, Hog and Lardo. They had moved in a week ago, about the same time as Pongwiffy, and had already caused her no end of aggravation.

This seems a good time to tell you a little about Goblins in general. Then you can decide for yourself whether or not you would care to live next door to them.

The most important thing you should know about Goblins is this: they are very, very, very stupid. Take the business of their hunting night – Tuesdays. That's when they hunt. It's Traditional. Whatever the weather, every Tuesday they all troop out regardless and spend from dusk till midnight crashing about the Wood hoping to catch something. They never do. It's common knowledge that the Goblins are out on Tuesdays, so everyone with any sense stays safely indoors and has an early night.

The Goblins are always surprised to find the Wood deserted – but they'd never think of changing their hunting night to, say, Thursdays, thus catching everyone unawares. That's how stupid they are. Of course, you could forgive them their stupidity if they weren't so generally all-round horrible.

After the futile hunt, Goblins always have a party. The party is always a flop, because there's never anything to eat, and invariably ends with a big fight. Goblins like fighting. It goes with their stupidity, and the Tuesday night punch-up has now developed into a Goblin Tradition. It's a silly one – but then, all their Traditions are silly. Here are a few more, just to give you the idea:

Painting Their Traps Bright Red; Bellowing Loud Hunting Songs Whilst Walking On Tiptoe; Stomping Around In Broad Daylight With Faces Smeared With

Soot, so they won't be noticed; Wearing Bobble Hats, even in a heatwave, To Stop The Brains Freezing Up; Cutting The Traditional Hole In The Bottom Of The Hunting Bag, so that whatever goes in immediately falls out again.

Right, that's enough about Goblins in general. Let's now get back to the Gaggle in the cave next door to Pongwiffy.

All Goblins are great music lovers, and Pongwiffy's new neighbours were no exception. They kept her awake at all hours, playing ghastly Goblin music at very high volume. Goblin music sounds rather like a combination of cats trapped in boxes, burglar alarms, and dustbin lids blowing down the road, so you see what she had to put up with.

It was most unfortunate, then, that the Gaggle Next Door chose the very night that Pongwiffy was entertaining Sharkadder to supper to hold their Official Cave-Warming Party.

Just take a look at the following:

       7 Goblins make a Gaggle

       3 Gaggles make a Brood

       2 Broods make a Tribe

       1 Tribe makes life unbearable.

The Gaggle next door had invited no less than two entire Tribes to their cave-warming – and that, if you can't work it out for yourself, is eighty-four Goblins!

They all arrived at the same time, singing. Can you imagine?

> *'A hundred squabblin' Goblins*
> *Hobblin' in a line,*
> *One got stuck in a bog, me boys,*
> *Then there were ninety-nine . . .'*

they howled joyfully, pouring into the cave. Next door, Sharkadder leapt from her cardboard box, sending the plate of skunk stew crashing to the floor.

'My new neighbours,' explained Pongwiffy, scooping the spilt stew on to her own plate. 'I'll eat this if you don't want it.'

> *'Ninety-nine squabblin' Goblins*
> *Hobblin' out to skate,*
> *One went under the ice, me boys,*
> *Then there were ninety-eight . . .'*

warbled the Goblins relentlessly, stomping around in their hobnail boots and beating their warty heads against the wall. A small avalanche of stones rained down on Sharkadder's new hairdo. A large spreading crack indicated that the ceiling was about to fall in.

'Stop them! Stop them making that dreadful noise!' howled Sharkadder, trying in vain to protect her curls.

'Ninety-eight squabblin' Goblins
Hobblin' down to Devon,
One got chased by a bull, me boys,
Then there were ninety-seven . . .'

droned on the Goblins, and Pongwiffy's favourite
poison plant keeled over and died on the spot.

Then the ceiling did fall in. There was a groaning,
grinding noise, and down it came with a huge crash,
burying both Pongwiffy and Sharkadder under several
tons of rubble. Luckily, they're Witches – and Witches
are tough.

'Sharky? Where are you? Are you all right?' called
Pongwiffy, crawling out from under a large slab of
granite and peering through the murk at the fallen
boulders littering the floor. There was a moment's
silence. Then the overturned cauldron gave a heave,
and Sharkadder emerged, shaking with fury and covered from head to foot in skunk stew.

'Oh dear,' said Pongwiffy. 'Sorry about that.'

'I'm never speaking to you again, Pongwiffy!' hissed
Sharkadder, and she ran weeping from the cave.

PONGWIFFY

Kaye Umansky

Look out for more laugh-out-loud stories about
Pongwiffy – a witch of *very* dirty habits!

If you have any difficulty in finding these in your local bookshop,
please visit www.bloomsbury.com or call 020 7440 2475
to order direct from Bloomsbury Publishing.

THE DAILY MIRACLE

It's a miracle!

Following much pestering from our readers, *The Daily Miracle* will now be available to view online at www.pongwiffy.com Head here to keep up to date with all of the news from Witchway Wood

Crash 'n' Bang rocks Battle of the Bands

Miss out on the washout show from the Witchway Rhythm Boys? Luckily a pixie at the scene managed to record some of it – go to www.pongwiffy.com to listen for yourself